THE STRAN

'Leave this house at once. Sir Hayden has already been too generous. Do not dare to come here again. If either of you should be so bold, I will set the dogs on you as I would on any skulking vagrant who ventures on to our property!'

I was white and shaking. Nothing I had ever heard from my mother had ever led me to expect this. But I was angry, too, with a burning flame of hatred that I could not control. I could have killed her.

'As God is my judge,' I cried, 'I will rise as high as you one day, and when I do I will use everything in my power to hurt and insult you as you have hurt and insulted me today!'

**Also by the same author,
and available in Coronet Books:**

My Sister Sophie
The Dark Tower
Time Of Dreaming
The Devil's Innocents
The Dancer's Daughter

The Stranger at the Gate

Josephine Edgar

CORONET BOOKS
Hodder and Stoughton

Copyright © Josephine Edgar 1973

First published in Great Britain 1973 by
William Collins Sons & Co Ltd

Coronet Edition 1976

---

*The characters and situations in this book are
entirely imaginary and bear no relation to any real
person or actual happening*

This book is sold subject to the condition that
it shall not, by way of trade or otherwise, be
lent, re-sold, hired out or otherwise circulated
without the publisher's prior consent in any
form of binding or cover other than that in
which this is published and without a similar
condition including this condition being
imposed on the subsequent purchaser.

Printed and bound in Great Britain for
Coronet Books, Hodder and Stoughton, London,
By Cox & Wyman Ltd., London, Reading and Fakenham

ISBN 0 340 20774 4

CHAPTER ONE

It was still dark when I awoke in the stuffy cottage bedroom with my mother asleep in the bed beside me. Along the road the knocker-up came hammering at the cottage doors, and presently there was a clatter of clogs as the cotton-mill workers left their homes and our landlord and his son and daughter stumbled downstairs to the kitchen for a bite before they left for work.

I snuggled down beneath the blankets with a sense of comforting superiority — at least Mother and I were actresses, a cut above these poor labouring folk who were glad to take our money for a room. And I was more than that: until my father had been killed six years ago I had been a lady born. Miss Sarah Maria Sefton, the daughter of Sir Gore Sefton, Baronet, of Rollers Croft Hall in the county of Derbyshire. The spoiled and indulged only child of a proud and reckless man. A man of strong passions and stubborn and, indeed, often cruel decisions. When his only brother Hayden and his wife Charlotte refused to accept my mother, an Irish actress from the London theatre, he never spoke to them again during his lifetime, and made no allowances to them from the family estate, leaving them, and their twin sons, to manage as well as they could on Hayden's army pay.

I had never met these cousins or my aunt and uncle. But I still remembered my life at Rollers Croft Hall very well. On the nights I was not playing at the theatre, alone in bed before my mother came home, I would pretend I was back there again, and that my life since my father's death had only been an unhappy dream.

I had had my own rooms, my own nursemaid, my own pony. My father had called me his little jewel, 'braver than any lad', taking me riding and driving in his high-wheeled chaise behind the spanking trotters, giving me gifts, telling me that even if my mother was a play-actress I should marry as well as any girl in the country one day. I think now it was bravado, pretending I was as good as the son my mother did not have, and better than Hayden's boy twins. But I was a child then, too young to know that the estate was entailed to the eldest son.

Then one day Sir Gore was killed in a mysterious shooting accident and everything, title, house, money and position, went to his brother Hayden. My mother and I had to leave the Hall. My mother, who had always been beautiful, gay, lazy and spoiled, became nervous, timidly apprehensive, inclined to drink her troubles away.

She blamed these troubles, not on Sir Hayden, but on his wife. Nothing was ever my mother's fault.

'Because I was pretty and she was a tall stick of a girl, and Gore never so much as glanced at her and because I was an actress and she, God save us, distantly related to an earl, she always hated me. Looking down her long nose with those cold eyes. Faith, we're all God's creatures, Charlotte, I told her, but she never answered. That was the day Sir Gore sent her and Hayden packing and I never saw her since. Sure I asked him to let them have some money, but he would not, for he was a hard man, and his pride had been hurt by Charlotte's insults. That was before you were born, Alannah, and I've never seen either of them since. When Sir Gore was killed and Hayden inherited I was told to leave at once. Tit for tat. Charlotte had her pound of flesh.'

But the Seftons did not leave us quite destitute. They allowed my mother a tiny income, sent to her through a lawyer, on the condition we never approached them and never used their name in any way. It kept us this side of respectability.

The stage was the only profession my mother knew and necessity forced her back to it. But the beautiful young comedienne had gone for ever — the tragedy of my father's death had broken her. She was illiterate and had to learn her parts by rote. I would sit reading them to her by candlelight while she tried desperately to commit them to memory, but her confidence was gone, and increasingly she drank and had now sunk to playing in a set-up company, Maestro Roland's Royal Travelling Theatre — an impressive title for a shabby troupe of mountebanks going about the provinces with their props and tawdry costumes in wagons setting up our tent in fields, inn-yards or barns.

Ashamed of this she took the name of Thring, her mother's maiden name, and did not use her own, Molly O'Brien, under which she had once been known as one of the prettiest young actresses in London. Now I was sixteen, a pale, undersized slip of a girl, and had started playing small parts. I was given fairies, columbines, and child parts and with my thin face and big eyes I did very well as a martyred innocent. Little Sally, The Child Wonder. I hated it, knew we were in the slums of the profession, and longed for my old life at Rollers Croft Hall.

Now, for the first time in our travels, we were near to Rollers Croft, the great house which I always looked upon as my own real home. Maestro Roland had set up the theatre in the barn of The Bear and Bell Tavern just outside the town of Matlock. I told my mother excitedly that we were very near our home — only ten miles away across the fields, little more than two hours' journey by road.

She sighed and said, 'Ah, sure it might as well be in the deserts of Turkestan for all the use it is to us. If you'd been a boy, now, my darlin', we'd have been queening it there still, and Hayden and that long-nosed bitch Charlotte still living on a captain's half-pay. Or maybe not, for I'd never have been as hard on them as they have on me.'

Off the stage she spoke in a rolling Irish brogue. It was quite different from her lucid stage diction. Her only school had been the stage. She taught me to speak, to place my voice, to sing, walk and dance and act, and she was a good teacher although she could neither read nor write. But I told myself I would not need to be an actress, for one day our old life would come back again — and now, when we were so near to the Hall, I was possessed with these dreams.

Surely Sir Hayden and Lady Sefton could not really be such

monsters. I knew my mother could not help her extravagant lies and that my aunt and uncle, county people as they were, could have found her free ways and language offensive. But I could behave like a lady. It was near to Christmas, the time for reunions and reconciliations. Surely if I went to my uncle and aunt and told them of our hardships they would relent and take me back into the family.

I was imaginative. I had vague plans of settling my mother in a rose-grown cottage near enough for me to visit but not near enough to embarrass our important relations.

'I am refined,' I told myself, staring at a strip of cold, starfilled sky between the bedroom curtains, 'and well-spoken. And I know how to be pathetic.' And then I laughed under the blankets, because if I had inherited pride from my father, I had laughter from my mother, and, playing orphans and martyred children, knew how to wring heart-strings.

I'll make them sorry for me, I thought optimistically. Anyway, I'll give them one more chance to be generous, in spite of what Herself says about them.

Herself, as the company called my mother, was deeply asleep. There was the sweet, heavy smell of laudanum, which she sometimes took when the black despair came over her and she could not sleep, or if she did she cried out strange words, asking for forgiveness and begging Sir Gore to return from the dead. But now she lay with her beautiful arms on the coverlet, her pretty hair once so fair and silken now coarse and dyed, her poor ravaged face temporarily at peace. She had once been called the prettiest woman in London and, green room wits had added, the silliest. I drew the covers over her arms and shoulders and kissed her. I hated her because she had no pride but she was all I had and I loved her devotedly too.

I rose, shivering, and lit a candle, poured the icy water from the ewer into the basin and washed. I dressed in my rough black stuff gown, boots and black poke. Over it all I put on a thick grey woollen shawl like the factory women wore. I hated the clothes but they were all I had. I did not realize what a skinny little waif I looked.

The landlady gave me a snap and a drink of milk and I told

her to tell my mother I would be back that evening. I put on my best stage manner.

'I have relations in the district and thought to walk over and call,' I said, and was gratified when she bobbed a curtsy and told me if I was taking the main Derby Road I would like as not pick up the carrier's cart as it was market day.

'What would he charge me?' I asked anxiously for I only had a few coppers.

'Aye, nowt to a little lass like thee if you'll sing him one of your songs.'

'Mrs. Dobbs,' I said with dignity, 'I only sing on professional engagements.'

I hurried along the mean street. The ice crackled in the puddles beneath my boots and above the crags the stars shone with a fierce, bright light. In the houses of the better-off folk lights were being lit as the servants got up and started the fires. I came on to the main road and passed the mill, alight and humming with spinning machines. The sky was grey when I heard the clop of the carrier's cart, and stopped to hail him. I was not afraid of the loneliness of the roads – for I was used to travelling, and too poor to tempt robbers. But beyond that I had this belief in who I was and what I really merited.

The carrier stopped and I crowded in between some country women going into market, with baskets of eggs and plucked and drawn birds. We toiled slowly along into the dawn. Some of them recognized me, having seen me in the show, and were inquisitive, asking questions about theatre life, but I soon froze them off with my wide-eyed stare. I have very strange eyes. Large, grey-green, sloping downwards at the corners and fringed with thick, dark, curling lashes. I had discovered that if people were impudent or annoyed me, to stare straight at them, and open my eyes very wide, usually silenced them. It was a stage trick, of course, but it gave me confidence. The women subsided and dozed over their baskets.

It was an hour later when the carrier stopped to let me down at the corner of the road that led up to the moor where Rollers Croft Hall was situated.

I told the man to look out for me on the return journey, adding importantly that I had to play with Maestro Roland's Company that night, for although I loathed the life, I liked the attention that being a player gave me. I gave him a playbill out of my pocket, for we all had to carry some and hand them out wherever we were to try and fill the seats at night. He laughed and said good-naturedly that I was a proper young madame, whipped up his horse and left me standing in the chill morning air. I started to walk up the steep moorland road. Before my father had died I had always ridden in a carriage when I went abroad. I had forgotten how long this road was. I toiled onwards and upwards, looking anxiously across the fields at every corner, expecting to see the house. But it was a long way — at least five miles, and my face was hot and my boots hurting by the time the entrance gates came into sight.

Although it was still very cold, with a biting easterly wind, the morning sun was high as I came up to the entrance gates. Two stone pillars topped with carved armorials flanked the big wrought-iron gates at the entrance to the drive which wound away between a double avenue of elm trees. The Hall could not be seen from the road, but there was a pretty stone-built lodge house just inside the gates. When I had lived at the Hall it had been kept by a Mrs. Ridstone. Her husband had been my father's chief stableman in charge of the hunters and carriage horses, and their daughter, Gilly, had been my own little nursery maid.

Just before I reached the entrance — I was about twenty-five yards away — a closed carriage with two high-stepping bay horses came jingling out of the drive. It was a fine equipage with gleaming brass and polished panels, the doors bearing small painted crests. A liveried coachman was on the box.

I stepped on to the grass verge as the carriage passed and from the inside saw two young faces gazing down on me. A charming, delicate-looking boy of my own age, muffled up in scarves, a beaver hat pulled down on his thick fair hair, and a pretty, rosy-faced young girl about twelve, who looked somehow very happy and excited, as though the journey was some specially anticipated treat. In the seconds they took to pass we stared at each other, and then the carriage rolled away down the road. I watched it until it was out of sight and before it reached the bend in the road I saw that both the young people were peering out at me through the small pane in the back of the hood. Impulsively, forgetting my poor rough clothes, I waved. The two faces instantly vanished and the carriage rounded the corner out of sight. I had forgotten I was too poor and shabby to be noticed by rich young people.

I went on, through the side wicket in the now closed gates, and knocked at the door of the lodge. Mrs. Ridstone opened it. She looked just the same with her round, rosy, rather anxious face and her spotless mob-cap and apron. She looked at me enquiringly.

'Don't you know me, Mrs. Ridstone?'

Her hands flew up in amazement. 'It's niver Miss Sarah!'

'Yes, it is. So don't look as though you've seen a ghost.' Suddenly the tears were running down my face, 'Oh, Riddy, I'm so glad to see you again.'

'Miss Sarah ... I niver thought to see you again. It must be six years since you and Lady Molly left. There, there!' She patted me comfortingly and led me through into her kitchen, tiny, clean and brass-bright as a caravan. 'There's a good fire. Come and get warm. You'd like a bite to eat ...' She busied herself making tea and cutting bread and butter, and a slice of ham. 'Whatever brings you to the Hall ...' She stopped, her anxious glance suspicious. 'You won't try to see her present ladyship, will you? I wouldn't if I were you, miss. I don't think it would do.'

'What do you mean?' I gave her my specially defiant stare, hoping she realized that the spoiled little girl who had left the Hall was a grown young lady now. Well, almost grown.

The woman glanced away evasively. 'Well, Miss Sarah, Ridstone and I were glad to keep our jobs here, we were the only servants Sir Hayden kept on. And our Gilly too — she's maid to Miss Felicia. But her ladyship did say ... well, she did say, and you mustn't think I think it's right, but we do have to think of our position ...'

'Well, *what* did she say?'

'That on no account was we to get in touch wi' you or Lady Molly if we valued our places.'

It was like a smack in the face, waking me from my hopeful dreams, even a servant was forbidden to speak to us. But I was warm now, and the new bread and fresh butter were delicious. I said quietly, 'Who is this Miss Felicia?'

'Miss Marsden — she's a ward of your uncle's and has always lived with them. Before they came here. Sir Hayden and her dad were soldiers together with the great duke out in Spain, but he were killed there, and her mother died soon after. She's been with Sir Hayden and m'Lady since she was a baby.'

So they had been kind to one orphan — perhaps I could persuade them to be as kind to me. I began to gain heart, although I found the continual talk about *Sir* Hayden irksome. *My* father had been the baronet, the elder brother, and my Uncle Hayden had only been Captain Sefton, with whom my father had quarrelled over my mother.

No member of the Sefton family had ever visited us when I had lived at the Hall. Nor indeed any of the neighbouring gentry. The company at Rollers Croft had been my father's men friends, hunting men who stayed late, drank deep and played high, and occasionally my mother's raffish, witty friends from the London theatre. If people would not accept my mother, then, Sir Gore had said in his brusque and overbearing way, they could dam' well keep away.

'Is she a prettyish girl with curly hair?' I asked. 'In a red pelisse? The one I saw driving out just now?'

'Aye.'

'Who was the boy, all wrapped up in shawls?'

'That's Mr. Denby — he's delicate and m'Lady fusses about him. He doesn't go to school — he has a tutor here. They have gone to Derby to meet Mr. Jonathan who is coming back from school for Christmas. He goes to that school at Repton.'

'I see.'

I rose, put on my ugly bonnet and wrapped my thick shawl about me in a superior manner which I was far from feeling. And it must have looked ridiculous in such a shabby little creature. But I was Sarah Sefton and I was determined to live up to it.

'Is my aunt in residence?' I asked grandly.

'Aye, but Sir Hayden's away and will not be back today. And the young folk won't be home from Derby until afternoon.'

I only had to face one of them but I knew she would be the most formidable.

'Well, you need not worry, Riddy. I won't say anything about being here or speaking to you. But I am going up to the house and I shall see my aunt and — and explain our position to her. If they can help Miss Felicia Marsden, who is no relation, surely they cannot see their own flesh and blood in the position Lady Molly and I find ourselves in now?'

'I beg you not to, miss. It will only cause upset and unhappiness.'

I hoped my cool stare would put Mrs. Ridstone in her place.

'Nevertheless,' I said, 'I am going up to the Hall.'

I marched resolutely out of the lodge and started along the drive. It was wide, and the wind howled dismally in the ancient elm trees under the cold, bright sunshine. I felt a little better for the food and rest, but I had come a long way and was very tired. I did not fully realize what a poor, shabby little thing I looked.

It took me about half an hour to reach the top of the rise where the broad vale began to drop westward towards the Derwent and from where, at last, I could see the house again. Rollers Croft Hall, where I had been born and had lived for the first ten years of my life. Only two stories high, built of trimmed stone like a great E without the centre stroke, the south front had four semi-circular bays and looked out on the sloping gardens, orchards, paddocks and grazing fields. Seeing it again, the tears came to my eyes and I saw myself, a little girl in spotless muslin and ribbons, flying along the terrace to be caught up in my father's arms. All gone now — all finished through a stupid accident. It was not fair.

I hurried along until the drive ended at the wide stone-paved courtyard of the north front, sheltered on either side by the two wings. A long colonnade ran right round. Had it always been so enormous? I felt small, like some little insect, as I crossed this great space towards the main door.

There was a large polished brass knocker and a long iron bell-pull. I took hold of the handle and tugged it and the bell clanged in some far-away corner of the house. Presently I heard the measured steps of a servant crossing the marble-paved hall inside and the door opened. I knew that he thought from my thick boots, grey shawl and common black poke bonnet I should not be at the hall entrance.

'Yes?' he said.

'I wish to see Lady Sefton.'

'Indeed. What is your business, young woman?'

I wrapped the shawl round me as I had seen my mother do when playing high-born ladies, opened my eyes to their widest. I wished I was taller. I wished I could look down on him.

'My business is private, my man,' I said sharply, 'Will you tell her ladyship Miss Sarah Sefton wishes to speak with her.'

Astonished and with no further protest, he let me into the vast hall paved with black and white marble where I had so often played as a child. I waited while he went to announce me.

I glanced uneasily about me. Nothing had been changed, the portraits, the patterned arms, the old rich furniture. In an enormous fireplace with the stone-carved over-mantel a log fire burned and two big hounds stretched before the blaze.

'Benbow,' I said and one of them raised a grizzled head and then lay still again. The old dog who had followed so faithfully at my father's heels could not remember me.

The manservant returned.

'M'Lady will see you now,' he said. 'Will you come this way, miss?'

I followed him along the familiar corridor into the little parlour, the pretty, cosy room where my mother had idled away her days among her silks and frills, waiting for my father and the other gentlemen to come back from their field sports and amuse her.

Then it had been all rococo, cream and gilt and rosebuds. It had been redecorated and was now hung with a sombre red brocade. Over the marble mantel, where once Lawrence's portrait of Herself as Perdita had hung, was a large painting of two small boys. Both blue-eyed, one fine-drawn and very fair, a little remote, watching his sturdy, brown-haired brother who, with eyes narrowed and commandingly raised hand, seemed to be reprimanding the great hounds I had just seen in the hall, which, in the portrait, assumed a suitably fawning and cowering attitude before their fierce young master. The darker boy reminded me of my father, the attitude, the arrogance of the narrow blue eyes. I knew these must be my twin cousins, Jonathan and Denby, now no longer small boys but youths, two years older than myself, who must be at the end of their schooldays.

Lady Sefton stood by the window, a tall woman in a rich dress of dark green, a little old-fashioned in style, with fine lace about her throat and wrists. She wore a lace cap on her jet back hair, which was drawn back severely from a centre parting.

On one of her fingers and pinning the lace on her breast were jewels that I had once seen my mother wear. Sefton heirlooms — my mother's personal jewellery had been pawned long since. She had no jewels now.

My aunt turned and watched me silently as I advanced into the room. She was very pale, forbidding, and her dark eyes were quite expressionless. I confess she frightened me. But my stage training came to my aid and I drew myself up proudly, then made her a curtsy. I wanted to make an impression. I hoped she would see a family likeness but I think any she saw was only to my mother, and she hated me for that. She just let me stand there in an intimidating silence. Every moment made me feel younger, smaller and shabbier. I realized that she was not going to speak to me, and it was for me to state why I had come. The inflated optimism which had brought me so far was fast deserting me. I must speak, or I should turn tail and run, and my pride would not let me do that.

'I am your niece, Sarah Sefton,' I burst out desperately. 'My mother and I are in the district. My mother does not know I am here. I thought I would come and see you . . .' my voice faltered to silence. Was this tall, forbidding lady never going to speak? But I had faced hostile, even drunken audiences and I knew

15

that an actress must never show that she is afraid: 'I had thought, ma'am, that you might not fully know our circumstances. My mother has not been so well of late and does not play in London, where the money is good ... the little money you give us barely pays our rents. I thought that if Sir Hayden knew he ... he might help ...' My voice was again trembling, for I had never faced any audience as hostile as this. I flamed at her motionless form furiously: 'I thought you would be ashamed that your niece should be dragged up in a common touring company among the worst of the profession, and that at least you would give me the gentleness that my position deserves!'

'Have you finished?' she said and the loathing in her voice killed all my dreams. 'Has that woman not made you fully understand? The property is entailed to the eldest son. You have no legal claim upon us. Against any wish of mine, Sir Hayden chooses to make you an allowance. You are fortunate in that. That is all there is for you. How dare you come here with your play-acting whining and dramatics! Has your mother not caused us sufficient shame?'

I was not going to cry — nothing she could do or say would make me cry. My pride twisted within me into a fierce, painful knot. I did not understand why she should treat me so but my hatred of her grew to match her own. I was only sixteen — my foolish dreams were smashed and my voice broke as I cried, 'In God's name, madame, what harm has my poor mother done that you should feel so?'

'Harm? She came into our lives and brought hatred, quarrelling and years of poverty and exile to my husband and myself. And finally she brought murder. Have you not asked your beautiful whore of a mother how her husband was killed?'

'She told me. A shooting accident.'

'So it was given out, and so we have let people think. We had enough to live down when we first came here. He was murdered. Duelling they call it, but it is murder in this country, and I call it murder. She helped the man who did it to escape to France — the man with whom she betrayed her husband.'

'I don't believe it. She has told me it was an accident. It cannot be true!'

'It is true and Rollers Croft Hall is my home now, where I live in peace with my family. The theatre trash and the gambling wretches have gone and decent gentlefolk are happy to be welcomed here once more. That time is forgotten in the county. I will not have you coming here to drag us down again.'

'But how am I to blame? If what you say is true I knew nothing of it — I was only ten at the time. I am your niece, however foolish and misguided my mother has been. I am Sir Gore's daughter and a true Sefton.'

Her look scorched me, and her voice held withering disgust. As though I was some unmentionable thing. But I stood with my head held high and met her fierce eyes, although my heartbeats were shaking me.

'Who knows what you are or who sired you? That French murderer, Danjou, or some clown of an actor. She was carrying you when Gore married her, although she told him some fool's tale that you were born before your time, and he was too infatuated to question her. Indeed I sometimes think she enchanted him. A slut — unable to read or write, only able to make men lose their heads about her.'

There was a passion in her voice far beyond my youthful understanding.

'She caught the finest man in Derbyshire and reduced him to her slave and then betrayed him — betrayed him to his death. I never speak of her — or allow anyone to mention her name to me.'

She turned away to the window, a trembling hand over her mouth, and then I had a revelation that it had been my father whom she had really loved and that was where the embers of her hatred glowed. She spoke over her shoulder, her voice broken, shaken with hatred.

'Leave this house at once. Sir Hayden has already been too generous. Do not dare to come here again. If either of you should be so bold, I will set the dogs on you as I would on any skulking vagrant who ventures on to our property!'

I was white and shaking. Nothing I had ever heard from my

mother had ever led me to expect this. But I was angry, too, with a burning flame of hatred that I could not control. I could have killed her.

'Madame!' I cried to that stiff, averted back, and my voice must have startled her for she turned as though suspecting that I might attack her. We stood there, facing each other, equal in hatred and pride. I caught a glimpse of my wild, white face in a wall mirror and scarcely knew that it was mine.

'As God is my judge,' I cried, 'I will rise as high as you one day, and when I do I will use everything in my power to hurt and insult you as you have hurt and insulted me today!'

I turned and walked out of the room, across the hall, out of the house, not knowing where I was going, through gardens, paddocks and fields, walking furiously as though possessed, burning with anger and hurt pride and hatred, and shock, too, and horror, for the one strong crutch to my pride these past six years had been that, whatever else I was — a poor player girl — I was my father's daughter, and nothing could take that away.

It must have been after midday when I came to the craggy ravine which marked the end of the Sefton property. A wild place with tree-grown cliffs and the river swirling in full flood far below. For one moment I stood on the edge looking down and the thought of throwing myself off crossed my mind. There was no escape for me into a more spacious and gentle life now; and there was nowhere for me to go but back to the cotton-weaver's cottage near Matlock, and to the tawdry theatre set up in an inn barn. To go back to Herself and get her to tell me the truth. I turned resolutely away.

'That's a play-actor's thought,' I said scornfully, 'Hoping Lady Sefton would feel remorse when the poor broken little body was found. How would her remorse serve me? I would be dead and not see it. I'll not throw my life away. I have a purpose now. To make that lady feel what I felt today until she yelps for mercy — that's what I'll live for.'

I had no idea how I would bring this about, but I promised myself fiercely that it would be so, however many years I had to wait for it to come to pass. I was terribly tired and had come much farther than I had intended. I threw myself down in some dried bracken in the shelter of a large outcrop of rock and wrapped my shawl about me and instantly fell asleep. When I awoke I was stiff with cold and the winter sun was low in the sky. I jumped to my feet. It was a long way back and if I missed the carrier I would miss the performance and Maestro Roland did not spare words or cuffs when he was angry. Besides, my mother would be frightened if I was late. I set off as fast as my stiff, tired legs would carry me, back across the fields, but skirting the paddocks and gardens.

I could still see my aunt's cold, dark eyes and hear her voice telling me she would set the dogs on me. But just as I came level with the orchards, now bare of leaf and fruit, the temptation to look at the house once more was irresistible. There was a cattle gate, two curved oak beams set in the wall so that people could pass through to the orchard, but it was too narrow for the cattle to pass. I went through and, climbing on a mound, looked at the house. On this side there were three wide fishponds where the beck had been dammed, reflecting the fire of the low winter sun; the pinkish stone of the house glowed, and every window glittered as though it was on fire.

I stood looking at it, and then heard the sound of galloping hooves. A big black hunter came cantering into the orchard, bearing three riders, three young people, the girl I had seen earlier in the day up in front, her brown curls flying, a big, handsome boy holding the reins, the tall, fair, delicate boy, who had also been in the coach, clinging behind. They were all laughing and shouting, and as I began to run towards the cattle gate they saw me and the big boy sent out a terrifying viewhaloo.

In a panic I started to run towards the gate, caught my foot in a tree bole, and fell full length.

I knew who they were — my two Sefton cousins, and Miss Felicia Marsden. I lay motionless with my eyes closed, thinking: Let them be frightened ... let them think I'm dead ... My bonnet had fallen off and my silvery fair hair was streaming over the wet grass.

'You damned fool, Jon,' I heard the fair boy cry, 'it's no poacher. It's only a girl ...'

The horse had been reined in; I heard footsteps, and someone lifted me gently so that my head was resting on a shoulder clad in thick broadcloth. I did not move.

'It's the girl we saw on the road this morning,' I heard Felicia say. 'Has she fainted?'

The boy who held me took my wrist and bent so closely over me I could feel his breath on my face.

'Her heart is beating. You are a fool, Jon. You might have killed her.'

Another voice blustered. 'How was I to know? What was she doing wandering in our orchard!' Then with a touch of condescending anxiety: 'She looks damned queer.' I felt a strong hand shake my shoulder. 'Come on, miss, whoever you are, wake up and don't die.'

I felt the boy who held me strike the hand away.

'Don't touch her. You've done enough damage, you crazy idiot!'

Then the big, strong boy's voice, again, but differently. 'What pretty hair she has. For a common girl she's quite nice to look at.'

The boy who held me said in a low voice, I think only I could hear it. 'She's beautiful — she's the most beautiful person I've ever seen.'

Thin, shabby, small and young — I had never thought of myself as beautiful before. My confidence was miraculously restored. I had a heady sense of power. But I could not hold out much longer. The desire to laugh was now nearly stifling me. I remembered the innumerable deathbed scenes I had played and lifted my long lashes slowly and looked straight into the eyes of the delicate-looking boy I had seen in the carriage that morning with Felicia Marsden. I knew now it was my cousin, Denby Sefton.

His face was so purely carved, and he had an expression of penetrating sweetness. He trembled as he held me as though he had never touched a girl before, or seen anything as beautiful as myself as I lay in his arms, for all my muddy grass-stained clothes and streaming hair. I smiled at him, and he smiled back, the blood flooding his clear skin.

And then because I could contain it no longer I began to laugh.

'Oh,' he cried in relief, 'you're better. I was so frightened. Were you teasing us, pretending to be dead?'

He rose and helped me to my feet. He still held my hand and I let it stay there. The girl sat side-saddle on the horse which was now quietly grazing. She looked at me with an expression of hurt, childish jealousy as the two handsome boys stood on each side of me and stared.

Jonathan was tall and strong as a young man of twenty. He had curly brown hair, a fresh skin, and narrow, brilliantly blue eyes. He reminded me very much of my father, Sir Gore Sefton. He was handsome, and yet I found his very strength and handsomeness repellent. I could not explain why — it was the feeling that he would get what he wanted whatever the cost. He was dressed in an elegant, long-skirted coat, an embroidered waistcoat, and a high, starched, fashionable cravat. Very much the budding young man of fashion. He stood watching me, faintly amused, his narrow eyes like two hard blue stones, not troubling to conceal his admiration. The child in me was frightened — the woman in me preened.

Denby picked up my bonnet and shawl.

'You are a wicked little flirt, pretending to be injured,' said Jonathan. He spoke in a facetious, patronizing way, not in the least angry. He put his hand in his pocket, and brought out a guinea. 'Here, you'd better buy yourself a new bonnet.'

I opened my eyes wide and gave him my famous, indignant stare.

'Jonathan, please,' his brother protested.

'If you were afraid then it serves you right,' I cried. 'It is you who are wicked. You did not care if I was dead or not. You only cared whether you would be blamed for it. Not a bit of remorse for my poor dead body lying there.'

It was not really funny, it was just the way I said it made it sound so, and as I looked with droll appeal from one to the other, they both burst out laughing with me. Only Felicia did not laugh, but sat watching me, puzzled, suspicious, the childish gaiety gone from her. It was quite plain that she adored the two boys; perhaps had been waiting for Jonathan's return from school with eager impatience. But now, at this moment, they only had eyes for me — the roughly-dressed stranger girl.

'I am very glad you are alive,' said Jonathan, his eyes never leaving my face. 'I just saw a dark figure moving beneath the trees and took it to be one of these poaching lads who are after my father's birds. Now say you're not hurt and that you forgive me even if you think me the greatest oaf in the world.'

He had not said he was sorry. He was still trying to cajole me. He expected me to give him some pretty reassurances and accept his guinea. But I did not. I turned away indifferently, and spoke over my shoulder with an insolence as stulied as his own.

'If you are an oaf, you said it yourself, and I am not going to deny it. You have certainly not behaved like a gentleman.' I looked at Denby and said apologetically, 'Was I really trespassing?'

He studied my face for a moment, then unexpectedly took out a clean handkerchief, and said, 'You have some mud on your face,' and as my hand went up automatically, with the same grave courtesy: 'No, let me,' and very gently he wiped the offending mark away. 'It was not trespassing,' he went on, 'just to walk through the property. What harm can that possibly do? You are very welcome to do so at any time. And if you cannot bring yourself to call my brother an oaf, to his face, I will, I promise you.'

His gentleness gave me a strange feeling. I had not thought to find it in my enemies. I had this feeling of having a choice, but of course, it was not as clear as that. It was as though I could forget my anger and sense of injustice now or follow my sworn path of resentment and revenge. But I remembered my Aunt Charlotte, his mother, who only a short while ago had said she would set the dogs on me like a beggar.

This house, these grounds, that fine horse — if I had been a boy, these would all still be mine, and they would be the beggars at the gates. I must remember this.

'Thank you,' I said, 'but I may not be this way again. I must go. It is getting dark.' I glanced round, dropped my voice sweetly with a theatrical touch, wanting to impress myself on their minds. 'I came because there used to be early violets here sometimes — in the south-facing banks. But it's too cold, of course.'

'You are like a white violet,' said Denby and did not seem to know he had spoken.

Jonathan roared with derisive laughter. 'Listen to my scholarly brother paying compliments. You have enchanted him.'

But he was jealous I could see. Denby started, flushed, and said gravely, 'You are shaken. You could ride the mare . . . or I could get a gig or carriage for you. Or shall we accompany you?'

'No, thank you.' I pulled on my bonnet and began to move towards the cattle gate. 'I can manage alone.'

'But who are you?' cried Jonathan. 'Do you live hereabouts?'

'We are Denby and Jonathan Sefton of Rollers Croft Hall,' said Denby. 'What is your name — where do you come from?'

I slipped through the cattle gate in the darkling light. There was a spinney of dark trees just beyond, and I went into them, hiding. I saw them rush forward, collide in the narrow gate, then Jonathan thrust his brother aside, and burst through. I nearly laughed aloud. Denby followed slowly. They stood there, peering round in the dusk, but my dark clothes concealed me. I called out, clear and bell-like through the gathering dusk, and my voice carried across the field.

'My name is Sally Thring and I come from nowhere,' and even as I spoke, I moved swiftly and silently, so, as they turned towards the voice, I had already disappeared.

Quickly I made my way back to the lodge. Ridstone was there taking his evening meal. He was a thin, taciturn man, and merely nodded when I came in. His wife saw my white face, made me sit down, and said, 'I reckon you didn't get much change out of m'Lady, then.' I felt the tears and turned my face away. 'Nay, love, I told thee it were no good.'

'It's true then — what she said?' I asked pitifully. 'About the way my father was killed? In a — duel?'

'Duel or murder, how should I know?' said Ridstone laconically. 'I heard the shots and saw these fellows wi' a carriage in the low meadow. They told me to look to Sir Gore, and then were off. I got a lad from the stable and we carried him back to the house on a hurdle. Your mother went on like a mad thing. When Captain Hayden came — Sir Hayden that is now — it was given out to be a shooting accident. We were the only folk he kept on. For all I know it was a shooting accident.'

'Did you see the other man?'

'A glimpse — handsome, dark, young chap. But you forget it, miss, for nothing can change things now. I'll get trap out and drop you down to the main road. You forget it, and don't come round here. We've got a good place and a snug home and we don't want trouble. Nowt can change nowt now.'

It can, I thought. Fate can. Death can. And *I* can if I set my mind to it.

He drove me down to the main road where I just caught the carrier jogging back from Derby. I slept all the way back, exhausted with emotion and my long day. I had set off with such high romantic hopes, and now I was creeping back to my mother and my sordid, insecure life, full of hatred, full of doubts about my parentage. I remember the country women, returning with empty baskets, woke me outside The Bear and Bell where I had asked to be put down. The flare lights were burning outside the yard entrance, and I heard the sound of the drum, and Maestro Roland's voice trying to entice the yokels in for the evening performance.

As I got down, I heard one of the women say, 'Ah, poor lass, she's nowt but a bairn after all.' And pulled myself awake.

The dressing-room for the ladies of the company was set up in a disused dairy at the back of the inn, cold and damp but better than under canvas at this time of the year. I went past the Maestro, who stopped his harangue long enough to curse me for being late, and went into the dressing-room. Tallow dips and a smoky brazier gave light and a little warmth. I was relieved that my mother was changed and made-up, and alone.

I went to her side and looked down at her. She was not drunk, but not quite sober. She caught my hand, looking up at me with eyes like a frightened child.

She could read in my white face and burning eyes that I had

learned the story of my father's death, and why we were banished from our home. All her life she had relied upon her prettiness and evasive lies to protect her, but now there was nothing she could say. The tears rose, as they did so easily with her, and ran blackly down her cheeks from her painted eyes.

I put my arms round her and held her fiercely.

'Don't cry,' I said, 'it's all right. We shall be all right in spite of the Seftons.' I felt her relax against me with relief, and drew a great breath, and went on: 'One thing she said — that woman said. She said I might not be Sir Gore's daughter. Mama, you must tell me the truth.' I felt her stiffen and draw away and look up at me. 'Am I?'

'The holy saints protect us, of course you are, my darling!'

'Will you swear it?'

'Of course I will.'

Her rosary hung on a nail by the mirror. She was a Catholic, but Sir Gore had not allowed her to bring me up in that religion. I took it and put it into her hand.

'Well, swear upon this that you have told me the truth and I am my father's daughter.'

She was trembling, she glanced at me in her evasive, pleading way, and said, 'I'll do that for sure, my darling,' and added in her deep theatrical voice, with the fine modulated accents she never used in real life: 'I swear that you are his daughter and only beloved child.'

I believed her. Suddenly I was very tired. But I had to make myself up and put on the grubby white frills and rosebuds and scarlet bows of Columbine. I tied my hair and began to grease my face.

'She said that you protected my father's killer?'

But Herself had recovered. She filled her glass, and said scornfully, 'Ah, that one, she would say anything to send me to the devil. It was no one's fault. A jealous quarrel. One man was already dead. Did she expect me to send another to the gallows?'

I stared at her, looking at her reflection, massaging her plump chin, pushing this old tragedy away like a piece of old rag.

25

'Ah,' she said, 'Gerard was no murderer. He was just a man out of his mind for love of me, like the pair of them were. Like bantam cocks. They didn't mean it to end like that.'

Once she had been so pretty and for a season London had been at her feet. Men had been crazy for her. Well, I was her daughter, and today two young men had thought me pretty. I could use my looks and my talent too. But I would not be soft and easily led. I would set myself a goal and go after it and that goal was Rollers Croft Hall. I sat still, looking at her through the mirror, the red grease-paint poised above my lips, my eyes wide and wild.

'Ah, don't be looking like that, Sally, my darling,' she cried, 'like the past has come back again to haunt us. Don't think badly of me now.'

I had this tender, protective love for her, my foolish, dear one. I rose, and kissed her, and I took the bottle away and hid it, and that night, after the show, when we lay in the flock bed in the labourer's cottage and she slid into her usual twitching, restless sleep I knew there could be no more dreams, I had to go up in the world, and the only road for me was the theatre — my only weapons my talent and my looks and these I had to use to get what I wanted from life.

CHAPTER TWO

The provincial tour ended at York in a burst of triumph. I was now twenty, and for the past four years had worked at my profession like a slave. Life had been good to me. I had grown from a skinny, pale, sixteen-year-old into a young woman of considerable poise and beauty. False modesty is no use in the theatrical profession where one's looks, voice, grooming and manner are assets to be calculated. I was not tall but slender and shapely, and I had learned to walk in a way which gave an illusion of height. Presence, Herself called it. My hair was very long, and silvery fair, and I had these strange, grey-green eyes with their slight downward slant and heavy, long-lashed lids — eyes that had no resemblance to my mother's round blue ones.

The company with which we were engaged ended the tour with two weeks in York. I was playing the 'juveniles' or *ingénues* as they were beginning to be called now the wars were over, and the rage for all things French had become fashionable again.

I had found my form that season — I was experienced enough to project my rôles as I wanted to and not to allow anyone, star or not, to upstage me. The northern audiences with their wide generosity towards a promising newcomer had taken me to their hearts, and the last week had been a great success. Bouquets, feastings, applause and a benefit of my own which brought me nearly £200. And also the offer of an engagement at The Royalty Theatre in London at the weekly salary of twenty-five pounds, a good offer for a young performer with no previous London experience.

Mr. Almeric Hodgson, the manager of The Royalty, had travelled north especially to see me play the classic parts of girlhood, Miranda, Perdita and Lady Teazle, and had offered me this engagement in town.

'I have excellent actresses in my company,' he said, holding my hand and gazing admiringly into what my admirers called, somewhat euphemistically, my mermaid's eyes. 'We can get actresses who are brilliant performers but cannot look young, and actresses who are young but whose talents are not developed. To find one who is not only a consummate artist but also the very breath of spring, the young Proserpine in person, that, my dearest young lady, is a most unusual thing.'

He had bunched his fat red fingers together and blown a kiss into the air of the green room, foetid with the theatre-smell of dust, candle-smoke and grease-paint. 'I prophesy a great success. The young gallants of the town will besiege the theatre. They will be stricken, dear child, as I am, with the penetrating darts of your lovely eyes.'

With which he leaned forward to kiss me, breathing brandy fumes like a red-faced dragon; I side-stepped adroitly and swept him a curtsy so all he managed to do was to bump his nose on my top ringlets as I rose.

I accepted the engagement with delight. It was good money. I knew I was pretty and a competent actress. I also knew that I did not act from the heart as the great ones did. I did not have that real magic. Acting to me was a means to an end — to make myself rich and independent. The only ways for a penniless girl to achieve these were the stage or marriage, and what opportunities had I for meeting eligible young men? One could become the mistress of a wealthy man, but this was not in my scheme of things. I had a purpose in my heart, forged four years ago when I had been rejected by my Aunt Charlotte at Rollers Croft, and this I hugged secretly to myself and never forgot. The stage to me was a way to my ambitions, not an ambition in itself, and I had brought myself and my mother a long way from the set-up in the barn of The Bear and Bell near Matlock, and Maestro Roland's company.

During the past four years, under my affectionate nagging and cajoling, Herself had greatly changed, perhaps because our circumstances had also changed as my earnings increased over the years. We had more security, could hire better lodgings, buy better clothes.

Since that day at Rollers Croft I had taken on the responsibility and planning of our lives. My mother rarely drank now, she was an impressive, pretty woman in early middle-age, and if she had gained weight it suited the parts she played, for now she was given what we called 'steadies' — those necessary but short rôles which almost every play contains, for although her appearance had improved, her memory had not. Her real triumph was off-stage, acting the part of my mother and chaperon. Neatly and modestly dressed, quiet-voiced and grave-faced, she was always at my side, discouraging the over-enthusiastic admirers who hung about the stage doors.

Alone in our lodgings or dressing-room we would go into fits of laughter over our escapades like a couple of schoolgirls. I was old for my age, far-seeing and shrewd, while she was an eternal child. I think the ten years with my father, Sir Gore, had done this to her, for his obsessional love had kept her isolated, spoiled and doted upon like a favourite odalisque or a rare caged bird. She could have had anything but her freedom; she had not to lift a finger; her only talents, those of an entertainer, went to waste. When he was killed, she was not only left without means but without a will of her own, or courage to face necessity. We complemented each other, shared our laughter and our troubles like sisters — but she would not share my ambitious dreams.

'Ah, Sally, my darlin',' she said once, wiping her eyes after one of our adventures, 'we should engage an old Heavy to play your father and set ourselves up as a family of aristocrats.'

'Which we are,' I reminded her. 'You may be billed as Mrs. Molly Thring but you are still Lady Molly Sefton.'

Her face darkened, and she looked at me uneasily.

'Ah, sure I thought you'd forgotten that old thing. I've put it out of my mind years past. Titles — what use are they to anyone? What good is it keeping up those old hates and memories? We're doing very well as we are — don't be driving me back to the drink with your high ways.'

'I will not,' I said, kissing her, 'But we must never forget that we really are Seftons. One day my chance will come to make the family remember us. I don't know how or when — but it will. You'll see.'

She muttered, crossing herself, saying I was foolish and sure weren't we happier without that nonsense. But it was not nonsense to me, nor had I any intention of forgetting my heritage.

But of course with work, success and fun, my dreams of revenge were not always in the front of my mind. I had a great many admirers. I had many invitations to routs, parties, picnics and race meetings which I only accepted under the most respectable conditions. Demurely dressed, with lowered eyes and gentle voice, my reputation spread until I almost rivalled the great Siddons in my staunch public virtue. Except that I doubt if Mrs. Sarah herself ever knew how to glance up under her lashes like I could, to hint at a promise of something behind a demure façade which kept the provincial gentlemen following in my train.

Now at last the farewells were said, our luggage was packed, and we were in the London stage-coach clattering down the Great North Road, the post-horns sounding as we went through the towns, chickens flying, locals staring, and I had started on my journey to conquer London.

Our trunks and boxes in the boot — it was a warm, damp spring day with the smell of newly-turned earth and violets in the air and my heart full of excitement and anticipation.

We were both dressed very soberly as befits two ladies travelling alone. My mother in brown with touches of a lighter velvet. Lately I had persuaded her not to dye her hair and when the colour grew out I realized why she had done this. Although she was still in her forties it was quite white. She told me it had been so since the day my father had been killed. But it was very pretty, and gave her a touch of dignity, useful both in her stage parts and her accomplished performance as my chaperon.

I wore a dress and bonnet of soft dove grey moiré, the bonnet was lined with white violets and I had a small tippet of good white fur. It was the most expensive outfit I had ever bought, but I wanted to make a good impression in London.

When I took my seat I was perfectly aware that all the inside passengers were looking at me and I hoped some at least knew of my recent success. I looked them over carefully to see if any would be of use or interest to me. There were a country couple, a parson, and a raw young Yorkshireman on his first visit to London who made sheep's eyes at me and went scarlet when I blandly stared through him as though he were invisible. As I did so, I found myself under an amused but tolerant scrutiny which to my annoyance slightly disturbed me.

The man who was watching me was in his mid-thirties, dressed extremely well in sober, legal black. A lawyer if ever I saw one. His thick, dark hair had a startling white wing on the right of his brow as though someone had brushed it with white paint. He had a handsome, humorous mouth, with a long, shrewd upper lip, very fine hands, well-shaped and well-kept with strong, long fingers. I suppose what caught my attention was not his good looks, for I had met good-looking men a-plenty, but the sense of power behind the formal legal façade. That and the deep resonant voice when he courteously greeted the other passengers. Lawyers, I knew, were always useful people to know, and he seemed quite charming, so I gave the merest hint of a smile in reply to his formal greeting which he acknowledged with a courteous bow and, again, the small, glinting smile.

The long road to London rolled endlessly past, through Doncaster, Newark and Grantham, and my feeling of elation and celebrity left me. After all I was only twenty and unknown in London. Herself went to sleep like most of the other passengers, except the lawyer man who presently asked me if I was going to London, and when I said yes, asked if it was my first visit.

'No, sir,' I said modestly, 'when my father died my mother took me to London and we lived there for a short time.'

'Your father has been dead for some while?' he asked.

'For ten years.'

'It must be very difficult for your mother and yourself.'

'It was very difficult, but of late our fortunes seem to have turned.' When he looked at me enquiringly, I opened my eyes wide and made the statement boldly, as I always did with obviously respectable people, daring them to patronize or look down upon me, 'My mother is an actress, sir. When my father died it was her only profession, and she has brought me up in it. I am going to take up my first London engagement at the Royalty Theatre.'

'Indeed,' he said, and his clean-cut, clever face took on a look of concern. 'Such a life must be full of temptations for a girl as young and beautiful as yourself.'

I smiled. 'If one is well-chaperoned it is not so difficult. One needs ...' I hesitated, and then said in a strong north-country accent, 'What Yorkshire folk call a right good head and no nonsense.' He burst out laughing, for as I had guessed, he was a Yorkshire man himself.

'And a great deal of charm too, I'm sure,' he said smiling.

I knew then I could trust him. A girl moving in a world of

men develops a sixth sense. The people I knew who were both kindly and of good position were rare. We introduced ourselves and I set myself out to charm and interest Mr. Robert Thornton to the fullest of my ability, and by the time we had reached our overnight stopping place, at the coaching inn at Stamford, we were good friends.

When my mother awoke he asked, very courteously, whether we would dine with him that evening, which we did very pleasantly. He was, as I had guessed, a lawyer. He had chambers in Grays Inn, and had been north to see a country client. He told us he was a bachelor, living in rooms above his law office, and from the competent manner in which he chose the dinner and ordered the wine he was also a man of the world. Although he took a private room for us to dine in instead of the noisy public room downstairs, he treated us not with the exaggerated respect which some men affect, nor with familiarity, but with natural good manners, and good humour which I appreciated very much. I thought how pleasant he was, how cool and clean, with his immaculate white linen. He was quick to laugh and to make us laugh.

I often supposed it was impossible for me to be seriously attracted to any man. The purpose in my heart would not allow it. But one day, when my plans materialized, I would need the advice of such a man, and one who respected and admired me would be more useful than any dried-up, snuff-taking advocate who thought of nothing but his fees.

So I was very gracious to Mr. Thornton, and when Herself, playing the lady chaperon very successfully, rallied him about being a bachelor, he said, 'if I had found anyone as charming as your daughter to grace my table, Mrs. Thring, I doubt whether I still should be unmarried.'

Up in our room, Herself, undoing her laces, and relapsing into her natural brogue said, 'Sure, you've made a conquest of that one, my darlin'. And a fine courteous gentleman he is an' all.'

I shrugged indifferently, 'He is very nice. He may be useful too. I might need a lawyer myself one day.'

'You could do a great deal worse than such a pleasant fellow,' said Molly. 'And I don't mean just as a lawyer.'

'I have no intention of marrying Mr. Thornton, so don't start your scheming and wheedling.' I slipped out of my dress, and pulled my long white nightgown over my head. 'I've only one ambition, so far as marriage is concerned, as you know very well.'

'Aye, I know,' said my mother disconsolately, 'To marry the Seftons' eldest boy and be Lady Sefton of Rollers Croft Hall. Sure, you give me the creeps the way you stick to that idea like a dog to a bone. It's impossible. And meanwhile you lose the chance of other good men when you've only this one mad dream in your head. I cannot understand you. You are clever, sensible and a great help to me — but this one thing rules you, and it's as mad as Bedlam.' She sat down before the small bedroom fire which the chambermaid had lit because the evenings were still cold, leaning her head on her hand, depression claiming her as it used to in the past. 'It brings all the old bad times back to me again.'

I sat before the mirror brushing my waist-length hair rhythmically, one hundred strokes, then rubbed it with a silk handkerchief to make it shine before I braided it for the night.

'Ah, Darlin',' pleaded Molly, 'Can I have a wee drop of something to send me to sleep then . . .'

I smiled, put on my woollen gown, rang the bell, and when the night waiter came ordered her a glass of whisky toddy. She was a great deal better, and if I was careful, and sweet to her, kept off both laudanum and spirits — but she still suffered from bad dreams. So I curled up beside her, and read to her by the candlelight, a cheap romantic tale of love and valour such as she loved, and she sipped her toddy, and presently was asleep.

In the morning we resumed our coach journey. When we approached the outskirts of London I looked out eagerly, for the city had been my goal for so many years. This was where I would find fame and fortune.

I had kept in touch with Mrs. Ridstone who was a widow now and knew the movements of my prey. The Sefton family had a town house in Mayfair and now both the twins had finished college and Felicia Marsden was of an age to be presented in society they spent a considerable part of the year there. They were in London at the moment, and Jonathan was a great buck, fashionable in the smart drawing-rooms and, I had been told, a frequenter of the theatre. I remembered the big, blue-eyed boy with his aggressive manner which had so repelled me and wondered how long it would be before we met again. Would he recognise me? I did not think so — but I would most certainly recognise him.

The city streets were dusty and crowded and I was dead tired as we drove through Moorgate. I had forgotten the press of traffic, carriages, tradesmen's vans and hackney coaches — the shouts of the drivers and street vendors, the smell of the piles of horse-droppings at the kerb side, buzzing with flies. At every crossing a bare-footed and ragged urchin swept a footway clean for the pedestrians.

When we alighted at The Saracen's Head which was the terminus for the northern stage-coach Mr. Thornton was very kind in securing our luggage and looking after us. He thanked me for my company on the journey.

'I have enjoyed meeting you,' he said. 'Is there any other way in which I could help you?'

I asked quickly if he could recommend respectable lodgings where we could take some rooms. My mother only knew the theatrical lodgings near Drury Lane where we had lived after my father had died, but I could remember the grubby lack of privacy, and the noise, and had no intention of going here.

His long, humorous mouth was unexpectedly kind.

'I shall be delighted, Miss Thring,' he said with a teasing mock humility. 'I was a little anxious about you. But it would have been presumptuous to show it, you are so obviously competent to look after your mother and your affairs. It's nice to know that you are only a very young girl after all.'

I was tired and his kindness hurt me. No one had looked after me for a long time — it was a hit below my guard, and for the first time in a very long while I felt sorry for myself in a stupid girlish way. I flushed angrily, and said I was sorry if I too had presumed, and I had no doubt we could stay at The Saracen's Head and find suitable lodgings next day.

'But I *shall* really be delighted to help you,' he said with grave gallantry. Not the trace of a smile although the long grey eyes still glinted teasingly. 'My daily housekeeper lives quite near my offices and I know she has rooms to let. She is an excellent woman, clean and capable, and a very good cook. I will drive you there. And then, if you will permit me, I shall be able to call occasionally and keep an eye on you.'

I had no intention that anyone, however well-meaning, should keep too close an eye on me. But I knew my touch of petulance had been out of place and ungrateful. I judged it was better to purr than to scratch with Robert Thornton. I did my best to look as young as possible, to call him sir and to dip him respectful little curtsys to remind him of my youth and helplessness. I had an uneasy feeling he was not in the least deceived.

But the lodgings were splendid. Two first-floor rooms, a bedroom and a living-room, clean and quiet, and moderately well furnished, and Mrs. Billings was both a good cook, and an admirable landlady. Mr. Thornton left us there with the promise that he would call the next day and invite us to dine, but against this I had a positive excuse. I opened as Perdita in two weeks' time at the Royalty, and my days would be so full of rehearsals and theatre business, that I could specify no free time, although, of course, I protested, I should be most grateful to him and always be delighted to see him.

He looked at me with a gentle cynicism, and said, 'You would make an admirable little lawyer yourself, Miss Sarah.'

'You are offended? I only spoke the truth.'

'I am sure you did. I can see a warning sign when it is given. You are happy that I am useful to you, but you do not wish me to presume beyond that usefulness.'

I saw my mother glance, and suppress a smile, and knew what she was thinking — here was someone who was not to be taken in by my blarney. I felt my cheeks flush and said, embarrassed, 'There seems to be a lot of talk about presumption between us.'

'Sarah—' again the use of my Christian name, but so kindly, not familiar at all — 'I am not a pestering stage-door idler, nor a pursuer of young girls. I have been happy to help you. If you are not interested in my friendship, I shall be sorry, but I shall understand.' He bowed to my mother, 'Good day to you, ma'am, and to you, Sarah, I wish you a great success in London.'

He made me feel thoroughly ashamed of myself. I put out my hands, frankly, catching his, forgetting myself completely in my anxiety to make amends.

He held my hands in a cool, strong grasp, and then let them go, and under his glance I really did blush like any unsophisticated country miss and I could not meet his eyes. He smiled and let go of my hands, and said, 'You're only a baby after all.'

'I am twenty,' I said defensively.

'And I am thirty-five. Old enough to know better than to be deceived.'

'Deceived?' I felt quite indignant. 'When have I deceived you?'

'You haven't — just for a moment, I deceived myself.'

I shook my head. 'You talk in riddles. Now I must retire early and study my part. But you will come and see us, won't you, Mr. Thornton?'

'My name is Robert,' he said, and his eyes still held that strange look, both tender and amused, the way people look at very young, silly, pretty things. It made me both confused and angry.

'I will call you Robert as though you were my elder brother,' I said solemnly.

'Oh, Sarah,' he laughed, 'what a little humbug you are. But I shall certainly come and visit you.'

When he had gone I forgot all about him. We had to unpack, dine, choose what to wear for my first appearance back-stage at the Royalty, and, as I said, to study my part. I was already word perfect. I never went to any rehearsal without knowing my words. But Herself, years ago, had been the rage of London in this part, with all the beaux of the Carlton House set at her feet, and I made her take me through it, line by line, until she was worn out, poor darling, while I pilfered every bit of business and meaning that I could adapt to my own interpretation and my very different personality.

The week was very busy. The red-faced Mr. Almeric Hodgson greeted me with much enthusiasm and a bouquet and opened a bottle of champagne when he introduced me to the company. But after that we settled down to serious rehearsal, and it was not until the following Sunday that I had a moment to myself.

Herself liked to stay in bed late on Sunday mornings, but I got up early and went to church. Not that I was very pious, but it was all to do with the impression I wanted to create in London. A good serious modest girl, who no one could take any liberties with even if she was an actress.

I put on my pretty grey dress, high-waisted in the fashionable manner, but with a quaker-like fichu of white muslin filling the neck. The latest mode was for large hats with plumes and ribbons, but I thought these were only suitable for tall and fashionable ladies. I did not want to look like an actress off stage. Was I not really an aristocrat? So I stuck to my demure little bonnet edged with frilled lace, and the brim lined with sprigs of white violets. After church I boldly summoned a hackney and was driven to Mayfair.

'My lady don't think local girls good enough for her two boys,' Mrs. Ridstone had written succinctly. 'She looks to grand matches for them both. Neither does she want young Jonathan to take up with Miss Felicia (for whom he has a kindness, although he's a right young scallywag now), Miss Felicia not having a proper fortune. And poor Sir Hayden ails, since he fell in the hunting field last year, and he is up there consulting the London doctors. So it's all quiet here at the Hall, with the family away in London.'

I told the driver to put me down at the corner of Farm Street and wait for me there. That last interview with my aunt when she had so insulted and threatened me was still in my mind, far more than the brief meeting with my two cousins when they were still schoolboys. I was not going to call and plead for help and recognition this time. But I wanted to see where they lived.

I walked quickly along Farm Street glancing up at the numbers. There were a few people about, obviously returning from the morning service. It was a fine bright day and this part of the city was clean and spacious compared with the noise and clutter of Holborn. I walked quickly, my glance modestly lowered, for I knew it was unusual for a young girl, as pretty and ladylike as myself, to be unaccompanied in the street, even at this hour.

I found the house, a tall brick building faced with stone, with a handsome doorway, flanked with iron sconces for torchlights. In the area at the servants' entrance a uniformed footman was taking the air and a sly pipe of tobacco, and glanced up as I passed. I went straight on, but I longed to bang on the polished lion-head knocker, and declare myself again, no longer a draggle-tail child in shabby boots and bonnet and a rough, coarse shawl, but as pretty and well-dressed as any rich Mayfair miss.

I walked to the end of the street then turned and retraced my steps. As I reached the house again a carriage drew up. The footmen came running out to put down the steps and two young people got out. I recognised them immediately.

The girl was Felicia Marsden, now grown into a tall, rather plump, English rose sort of a girl. The type of girl whose Papa takes a box for the theatre during the Christmas season — all brown curls, round blue eyes and high, well-bred little voice. She was dressed in blue silk with a small blue hat with a plume perched on top of her curls, very fashionable and not suiting her rosy round face in the least.

The young man was my cousin, Denby Sefton.

He was tall, slender and very fair. He was good-looking but still had an air of fragility about him. I think it was the delicacy of his skin and the shadows about his deep-set blue eyes. He was elegantly dressed, with a high cream-coloured beaver hat, and in spite of the warmth of the spring day, a loose cloak of warm tweed. There was something fine-drawn and sensitive about him — I remembered he had been an extremely delicate child, and that Mrs. Ridstone had said in her letters, that at Oxford, unlike his brother Jonathan, who seemed to have spent his time at university roistering and riding to hounds, he had been what she described as a 'champion scholard'.

They turned to help a thin, florid man down from the carriage. He must have been handsome once, but ill-health had drawn shadows about his eyes, giving him a haunting resemblance to the fair young man who hovered so solicitously about him. It was obvious that his back was affected and that he was in great pain. But he was too like my father for me not to recognise my uncle, Sir Hayden Sefton.

'Now, Father, lean on me,' said Denby anxiously, 'and Benjamin will take the other arm...'

But the sick man tetchily dismissed him.

'Get the other man... you're not strong enough, Denby. Get the butler fellow.' He sighed gustily, and said, 'The sooner I get out of this city and back to Rollers Croft, the sooner I will recover...'

I stood back, waiting for the small group to cross the pavement and go up the entrance steps into the house. In spite of Denby's protests and Felicia's anxious flutterings the butler was fetched, and the two manservants, with some difficulty, half-lifted Sir Hayden up the steps and into the house. I saw him grit his teeth and go white as they moved him. Felicia hurried after them.

Denby turned, raising his hat so that his thick pale hair shone in the sunshine, and began to apologise for holding up my progress. As he met my eyes the colour flamed up his fair-skinned face, and his eyes lit up.

'The white violet girl!' he exclaimed.

I summoned up my most freezing manner.

'I beg your pardon, sir, but I do not understand you. Will you kindly let me pass on my way?'

I began to walk on, but he remained by my side, hat in hand, his face tense with earnest, eager sincerity.

'Please believe me, I mean you no harm. You have been in my thoughts so often since that meeting. When we found that the name Thring was connected with the theatre company which was in the district, we drove over to the inn at Matlock, my brother and I, but the company had gone, and no one knew where. We have spoken of you so often together, wondering where you came from and where you went.'

I walked on silently, well aware that Felicia had come out on to the step and was staring after us in amazement.

'Please, Miss Thring.' He had even remembered the name I had called so mockingly in the twilight, 'Tell me where I can find you again. Don't just disappear again.'

'Sir, I am alone, and unprotected, and it is not gentlemanly that you should take advantage of me. I have no intention of telling you my name or where I live.'

'But believe me —' he was very moved, passionate and sincere: I was actress enough to know that here was no feigning — 'I respect you deeply. You said you came from nowhere once — don't go back there again without a word!'

We had reached the corner where Farm Street joins Berkeley Square. I was astounded to see, standing by my waiting hackney, the tall figure of Robert Thornton. He glanced across and immediately came across to us, lifting his hat to me in greeting, as though he had come to meet me. To my astonishment they were acquainted.

'Oh, Thornton,' said Denby, turning to him and grasping his hand, 'do you know this lady? If you do, will you introduce us? I met her once, some years back, when we were much younger. I know her name, but she says she cannot remember me. She will vanish again, and I cannot bear it. Tomorrow my father goes back to Derbyshire and I have to accompany him — I may lose sight of her for ever.'

He was so serious and impetuous that Robert Thornton had to conceal a smile. But he said very gravely, 'If Miss Thring does not wish to know you, Denby, it is not for me to go against her wishes.' He offered his arm to me punctiliously, but the long, clean-shaven lips were twitching upwards at the corners. 'Sarah, this is well met it seems. You will allow me to escort you home?'

I took his arm graciously, feeling very pleased with myself. Here was I, newly arrived in London, and one good-looking gentleman was beside himself to know me, and another was offering me his protection. But as I turned, something in Denby's sensitive face stirred me, some shadow, a premonition. I said, without thinking, 'I do remember you. But perhaps it would be better if you had never met me and never known my name. Let it stay that way.'

And then Robert handed me into the waiting hackney and took his place by my side, and the driver whipped up his horses round the square eastward towards Holborn. Denby stood on the corner, hatless, gazing after the carriage until we were out of sight.

Robert leaned forward, his chin resting on his hands, and his hands on his silver-knobbed cane, his long grey eyes quizzical.

'Now, young lady,' he said, 'will you tell me what all that was about?'

I opened my eyes wide and innocently. 'How did you come to be waiting for me?'

'Quite simple. I followed you out of church and saw you take a hackney. So I took another one and came after you. Miss Sarah Thring, I thought, is too young and too pretty to go wandering about London by herself. Besides, I wanted to ask you and your mother to dine with me tonight. But how do you come to know Denby Sefton?'

'Oh.' I shrugged. 'He's just a boy I met once, years ago. He — he seems to have remembered me.'

'He seems to be infatuated with you. This I can understand. But this is what I find strange — that you should choose to walk past Sir Hayden Sefton's house twice on a Sunday morning, and why young Denby Sefton, who is a studious and shy young man, should behave like this.'

'You know them? The Seftons?'

'Yes, not well, I have met them socially — but not often. They are very wealthy and move in more exalted spheres than I care to cultivate. Only a short while ago coal was found in great quantities under their Derbyshire estate. In Sir Gore Sefton's time they were Derbyshire squires, well off, but of no great estate. Now they are extremely rich. But what are they to you, Sarah?'

I looked at him, weighing up his feelings for me. Respect, I thought, for my youth and independence, and perhaps a light, paternal affection. I knew I could trust him and there was no one else I could trust. Herself loved me, but her tongue ran away, and she had neither wisdom nor discretion. I *needed* someone I could really trust.

'Robert,' I said, 'now I am in London, and earning a good salary I shall need a lawyer to look after my affairs. Will you accept me as a client?'

He laughed, and said, 'Most certainly.' He offered his hand, which I shook. 'But what has this to do with it?'

'Now you are my lawyer I can rely absolutely on your discretion,' I said triumphantly. 'Denby Sefton is my cousin. My father was Sir Gore Sefton. My dear foolish mother is legally Lady Molly Sefton, his widow.' And then, suddenly, as we jogged along Tyburn Way towards Holborn I told him about it — all about it, about my mother and father, the old antagonisms and quarrels and my father's tragic death.

He listened gravely, but I could see he was astounded.

'It sounds like a romance,' he said.

'But it is true,' I assured him, 'every word of it is true. I should have lived at Rollers Croft. My aunt and uncle should have looked to my welfare. I should not have had to struggle for my living on the stage.' And then I told him of that hateful scene with my aunt and her cruelty and scorn.

'And these two boys — your cousins, Denby and his brother? They do not know who you really are?'

'No,' I said and I felt my face going hard and cold, and my eyes sombre with that memory of my aunt. 'And I don't want them to know. Not until that woman begs my forgiveness. But I'll never forgive her. Not as long as I live.'

He looked at me curiously, and then leaned forward, touching my face with one of his long fingers. 'Sarah,' he said quietly, 'don't look like that. You are far too sweet and young to hate.'

His face held such concern and gentleness that I found my throat constricting and the tears filling my eyes. I would have liked to put my head down on his broad shoulder and cry. The last four years of work and endeavour, taking all the responsibility for my mother and myself, had been more of a burden than I had admitted and the unexpected touch and consideration unnerved me. But this was not in my plan — I had been able to do what I had done through these years with one goal ahead — that was somehow, in some way, to be in my aunt's position, and be the lady of Rollers Croft Hall. And the only way I could do that was through my cousins, particularly my cousin Jonathan, who one day would own it all. Nothing was going to deflect me from my purpose.

Robert said reasonably, 'As your lawyer, Sarah, I could investigate your position with regard to the Seftons. A legal approach might have more effect than a furious young lady bursting in on them out of the blue.'

'You can find out what you will,' I said indifferently, 'but I want no approach made to them until I hold the winning cards.'

'And that will be when your cousins are in love with you,' he said in the same grave rather unhappy voice, 'and one of them is already.'

'But it is the other one who matters,' I said. 'Jonathan — the eldest. But there is one thing you can do for us. You can write to Sir Hayden's lawyers and inform them that Lady Molly Sefton no longer wishes to receive the paltry allowance they have seen fit to grant her since her husband's death. But don't tell them why we can do without it. I don't want anyone to connect Sarah Thring, the actress, with Sarah Sefton, the baronet's daughter. At least, not yet.'

I met Jonathan again about a week later. *The Winter's Tale* opened, and I, as Mr. Hodgson had prophesied, made a great hit. I had been careful about my costume, not being too ostentatious as so many young actresses are, but wearing very simple, pale clothes, my long hair loose and natural, bound with blossoms. I knew all the regular actors at the Royalty were tried and experienced in their profession, and any impact I made must be of innocence and springtime, and I succeeded beyond all hopes. Perhaps because of Mr. Almeric Hodgson's meanness. The play was an old favourite, always in the repertoire, and he would not pay for a new production — so my fresh nymphlike appearance was enhanced by the tired old gilt palace in his pinchbeck Bohemia.

Because of my youth and comparative lack of experience, I tried my hardest to endear myself to the rest of the company, and most of them had been kind. Certainly the gentlemen had been kind — the ladies were more reserved.

My first entrance was well on in the play so after the success of the first night, Mr. Hodgson encouraged me to appear in the green room while waiting to go on, for it was there that all the critics and writers came, and if I pleased them they would give the play the puffs which were so valuable. Also all the smartest men about town came to meet the ladies of the theatre, and here all the scandals, love affairs and liaisons started.

But I was very careful. My costume of flowing draperies was revealing, but off stage I always wore a concealing shawl. And I always had Herself, in her richly sober gown and bonnet, beside me. If on occasions she forgot her rôle as a dignified chaperon and started to flirt with a handsome fellow, I would press my toe firmly on hers as a reminder, and afterwards we would giggle together like a couple of schoolgirls.

I did not see Robert, although he had been present on my first night, and sent me a gift of flowers. I had learned, through Mrs. Ridstone, that Jonathan Sefton was a great man about town, and worried his mother by his wild ways and his preference for theatre beauties rather than the carefully chosen girls of good family she would have him know. I had only to wait. Some time he would come to see the new young actress at the Royalty. I remembered him very well, the tall, handsome, impetuous boy, with the narrow blue eyes, and thick, curly, brown hair, but on the fourth night of the play, when I was holding my little court in the green room, and he did come, I was not prepared for his magnificence.

When I had seen him that brief, cold December dusk in the orchard at Rollers Croft, he had been a boy of eighteen. Now he was a young man of nearly twenty-three, tall, standing well above six feet, with broad shoulders and an easy arrogant manner, superlatively dressed, in an age when the king and his friends had set a standard for masculine elegance, but not an affected, drawling beau, like some of the men who haunted the theatre.

Mrs. Ridstone had said that my aunt adored this handsome son of hers and so did Sir Hayden. And I could well understand it. He came through the door with two other men, slightly ahead of them, like a young prince with his entourage. The secret, narrow eyes met mine, and once again I felt a rejection of him that was almost fear. I think it was because I had always been so free, always made my own decisions, and here was someone whose will was ruthless. A very young and very dissolute man who would have what he wanted from life, even if it was the merest caprice. He gave me the impression of dangerous violence held in extremely brittle control.

Mr. Hodgson, rubbing his hands with gleeful welcome, rushed forward to introduce us, and I curtsied formally, but did not give him my hand. I was actress enough to speak to him without blushing or trembling but my heart was racing, and I did not know whether it was because the meeting which I had planned for and dreamed of so long had taken place at last, or whether it was because, although I did not like him, I found him attractive. I knew that the other actresses there were watching us, wishing he was paying such attention to them. But I was certain of one thing — he was the enemy and I was certainly not going to fall in love with Jonathan Sefton. In fact, love was an emotion that I could not imagine between us. Passion, perhaps violence, but not love.

'Mistress Sarah Thring,' he said, and his smile and bow were condescending, and his bold eyes full of admiration, 'my brother Denby, before he left for the country with my father the other day, told me he had found our white violet girl again. Ever since I so rudely frightened you I have hoped that the chance would come for me to make amends. Will you not dine with me after the performance tonight, and try to forgive me for my bad behaviour?'

I did not answer him directly. I took Herself by the arm and presented her — she had not connected this handsome and arrogant young man with the Seftons, nor realised he was her nephew — but a flicker of apprehensive recognition showed in her eyes.

'Mama,' I said, 'this is Mr. Jonathan Sefton of Rollers Croft Hall in Derbyshire, which we know of old, don't we? Mama?'

She started, changed colour, curtsied, and I felt her fingers tremble on my arm.

Jonathan, disconcerted, glanced angrily at me, then back at his two companions. I knew their type well. Chaperons and mothers, unless they could be discreetly silenced, did not come into their plans for the evening. They hoped to find two other pretty young actresses to complete the party and drive off with us to Cremorne or Vauxhall or to a luxurious private dining-room somewhere.

Jonathan bowed ironically. 'Madame, may I have the honour of escorting your daughter to a small dinner-party which my friends and I are giving this evening?'

I pinched her arm gently beneath my shawl, our system of signals. Once for acceptance, twice for a firm refusal. I gave two distinct pinches.

'Sir,' she said with awe-inspiring Shakespearean dignity, 'I regret that my daughter is never permitted to dine with young gentlemen alone. Because we are of the theatre it does not follow that we have the morals of the streets. I beg you will excuse her.'

I saw the black fury in his eyes but before he could speak, the call-boy came in calling me to the stage, so I bade him an airy good night and went out on my mother's arm.

As we stood in the wings waiting for my entrance she was still trembling, and her eyes were filled with the old childish dread.

'Ah, don't look like that, Mama. You're not scared by a conceited young buck! I've seen you put such fellows down a score of times.'

'I hope you know what you're doing, Alannah. That's not one to play tricks with, even your pretty tricks. Did you see the way the eyes of him burned at you? He reminded me of times I was beginning to forget.'

I knew she was thinking of Jonathan's uncle, Sir Gore Sefton, her husband and my father, and remembering the violence that had ended her marriage ten years ago when he had been shot down in the fields near Rollers Croft Hall.

46

CHAPTER THREE

Jonathan Sefton's pursuit of me and my pursuit of him became a game of skill in which I was increasingly involved as the summer season went by, and a game of skill that was being watched and commented upon by fashionable London. I cannot pretend that I did not enjoy it. I had had a considerable success, I was accepted as one of the season's beauties, and one of the handsomest young men about town made no secret of his infatuation for me. Perhaps because my life at this stage was so hectic I began to rely increasingly on Robert Thornton.

His quiet rooms in Grays Inn were a refuge. I could go there alone without embarrassment or fear to talk with him, to ask his advice, to be quiet for a little while. The things about me that he liked were, I knew well, the true things. My capacity for hard and honest work, my tender love and consideration for my mother and, most of all, my impetuous youth. He laughed at me, and sometimes he was angry, but always wise, kind and tolerant. Sometimes as I walked with him beneath trees in the echoing courts of the old inn. I had the feeling of pure happiness and forgot all about planned roads of ambition and revenge.

I did not speak to him again about this – I did not wish him to know about the flowers Jonathan sent me; the expensive gifts which I always returned, the letters, never answered, with which Jonathan besieged me. I did not tell him that wherever I went — in the theatre, walking in London, dining or visiting friends — Jonathan would always be there, his narrow, dangerous eyes following me, his presence not to be ignored. I knew it was town gossip. I was told that bets were being laid in the St. James's clubs on which of us would capitulate, me by becoming his mistress, or he with an honest offer of marriage. Let the world of fashion laugh, I did not care, their gossip filled the theatre every night I appeared. I hoped the rumours had reached Lady Sefton's ears. I hoped she was anxious over the fact that her adored boy should be enslaved by a play-actress when she had hoped for a great match for him. We should see who would win this game in the end.

'I will wait for you for ever,' he wrote to me, 'I will never give you up. If I cannot have you no other man shall, that I swear.'

At first it had been flattering, and even amusing, but as the days passed I began to be a little afraid. I began to understand why my mother, so fundamentally more timid and simple than myself, had allowed herself to be swept away from the theatre by my father, and to be hidden away, bored and idle at Rollers Croft Hall. But I would not admit to any doubts — not even to myself.

Herself, richly and soberly dressed, nobly playing my chaperon, however late the nights and however tired she was, hated the whole situation. When we were alone she scolded me as she had never done before.

'Playing with fire, Sally, and you should stop before it is too late. I did it myself, when I was young. When a girl first feels the power of her beauty it goes to her head like wine . . . but I was silly and thoughtless, and there's nothing silly about you. You've a good head on your shoulders. It's all part of your foolish wicked scheming, and no good will come of it.'

But I kissed her, and said she was a nervous old goose, and I knew what I was doing, and that Jonathan Sefton might think he could have any girl in London because he was rich and handsome, but he could not have me.

'I have a price on my head, Mama, and he's going to offer that price.'

I would not listen when she reminded me of the tragedy of my father's death, and the young Frenchman Gerard Danjou who had fled from England never to be heard of again. All I thought of was Lady Sefton's insults, and my position, disinherited and disowned by my father's family. For four years now I had dreamed of this victory and revenge and now Jonathan's passion for me was putting it near my grasp. Curiously I did not think of Jonathan as a person at all. Not of his pride, nor his feelings — he was an object in my scheme and I did not care if he suffered.

I was free from the theatre for some weeks. A famous tragic actor, called MacFarren, was engaged for a season at the Royalty. He had elected to play Macbeth in which he was famous for making the rafters ring and blood run cold with his fearful ravings, and there was no part for me. I was grateful to have some free time to rest, as he had offered me a provincial tour, at a very good salary, and I needed a holiday. However Mr. MacFarren offered Herself the small part of Lady Macduff at a fair salary which we could not afford to refuse.

Every night during the run of *Macbeth* I went to call for my mother at the theatre. I took a hackney as I did not care to walk alone through the streets, although the summer evenings were light, because Jonathan Sefton would appear at my side if I did so. But when I came out this particular night the air was so sweet, the trees in Grays Inn and beyond in Lincoln's Inn Fields in full leaf of summer. A girl was crying lavender down the road, and I bought a sprig, for it reminded me of the paved garden at Rollers Croft, with the long lavender border humming with bees. I wished I dare walk to the theatre.

I looked cautiously about me, but could see no sign of the tall, waiting figure of Jonathan, decided to risk it and set off, meaning to go along Holborn and down Drury Lane, not wishing to risk crossing the seething slums of Clare Market.

I had not gone far when, glancing behind, I saw Jonathan's tall figure, the white hat set on the curly brown hair, the broad shoulders in the immaculate blue coat. Recently he had not accosted me in any way, for I would not speak to him. He would follow a little way behind my mother and myself, keeping his pace to ours. But now, for the first time, and foolishly, I was alone, and although I hurried in a few long strides he was by my side.

I turned and was startled and shocked by his expression and the suffering in his eyes. I had never been in love and, in spite of my surface sophistication, was very young — I saw desire and outraged pride in his tormented eyes. His obsession was out of my experience, beyond my understanding. I knew that this was no longer a game but a battle of wills, and because my only emotion was ambition at that moment I was the stronger. That I had this wilful, spoiled, passionate boy at my mercy. That if I held to my purpose I would win.

I stared up at him coldly. He was a great deal taller than myself. I did not speak. I became aware that a carriage had drawn up to the kerb, level with us.

He did not attempt to touch me, or take my hand. He was so moved he forgot the niceties of the foppish manners of our day. He neither removed his hat, nor bowed, nor greeted me, but spoke straight out of his frustration and pain.

'Sarah,' he burst out, 'you are driving me mad. I cannot rest for thinking about you. No other woman has ever possessed me like this. Am I so repellent to you that you will not even listen to me? I swear if you do you will not regret it. You are making me a fool before the whole of London society. I cannot go on like this. Will you let me drive you somewhere, where we can be alone, and talk? . . .'

We were at the entrance to Grays Inn — the carriage which was standing by the kerb had two men on the box, the driver and a flashily dressed young fellow, with the wide shoulders of a pugilist. He grinned down at me familiarly, typical of the bullies that fashionable young rakes employed as 'protectors' when they made scenes and fights in the gambling houses round Covent Garden. I was suddenly afraid — in his present mood Jonathan was quite capable of having me lifted into the carriage and carried off — a not unheard of thing among the fashionable and dissolute young men about town, although some of the young ladies so abducted were not at all unwilling about it.

I looked round, a little frantically, and saw with a rush of relief that Robert Thornton was just within the archway, walking with another lawyer, in deep conversation. I could put out a velvet paw again and tease this great mouse I had in my clutches.

I opened widely innocent and affronted eyes, and spoke to him for the first time in weeks.

'I have nothing to say to you, Mr. Jonathan Sefton. Your

intentions are abominable, and your attitude insulting. I think you must be mad to imagine anything would induce me to drive with you or trust myself alone in your company. I see that my lawyer, Mr. Thornton, is within the archway — I have come to meet him, and shall certainly tell him of the manner in which you have been persecuting me.'

I whisked round and ran through the arch, and then slowing my steps walked demurely towards Robert. I had not been to see him quite so often lately — I could never lie to him, and playing this dangerous game with Jonathan, I found this difficult. He saw me, bade his companion farewell, and came to my side.

'Sarah,' he said brusquely, 'what are you doing walking alone at this time of the evening?'

I looked penitent. I looked pretty too, I know, because I wore my new Indian muslin of patterned pink flowers, and a straw summer bonnet trimmed with roses. I never wore the mass of corkscrew ringlets which were now fashionable — and often false — but always had my silver-fair hair plainly parted, and wound into a knot on the nape of my neck. I played young innocents on the stage, and was adept in looking the part — although, of course, in spite of my schemes I really was innocent, and often very foolish.

'I am going to meet Mama from the theatre. And it was such a fine night, I thought I would walk. And I am already beginning to regret it.'

His observant glance swept the street, and I had little doubt that he had observed Jonathan in the shadow of the archway. He took my arm and said he would accompany me and I began to chatter, hoping to avoid any mention of Mr. Jonathan Sefton.

'You have been avoiding me lately, Sarah,' said Robert.

'No,' I protested, 'not deliberately, Robert. I am not working, and I have so much to do. I am studying a new part. Mr. MacFarren has offered me a provincial tour, to play several new roles with him. Desdemona, for instance.'

'The young lady who gets murdered by her jealous husband,' he said, glancing wryly at me.

I ignored this, but did not meet his eyes.

'And then there is sewing, and shopping for new clothes, and getting ready to travel — Mama is no good at such things. And writing for lodgings at the various towns. And going to meet her at the theatre.'

'You go every night?'

'Yes,' I said, then: 'She is a darling, but she has many bad friends. She is what people call good company. But for me she would stay late and get into bad ways again, and I don't want that. She is weak — and the past haunts her. She blames herself, and sometimes the black moods come on her, and then I stay close to her so that she doesn't slip away again into drink and despair like she did after my father was killed.'

He stopped suddenly — we had crossed Holborn and were walking through Lincoln's Inn Field.

'Sarah,' he said, 'there are times when I could beat you for your wickedness and selfishness. But there are other times when you are so sweet and loyal and kind that I can only think how very much I have come to love you.'

All my assurance vanished. I stood, my mouth open, gaping at Robert as though I had never seen him before. I had always known this man, who was such a fine and cultivated gentleman, was fond of me, but I had thought his regard something quite different. I had thought he looked upon me as a sort of pet, or perhaps a young and rather foolish sister; that he had a concern for my unprotected position and was wary about my impulsive ways. I had not thought of it as a personal attachment — not as love. Suddenly I felt choked with emotion, as though my breast was filled with unshed tears.

'Love me?' I repeated stupidly.

'Does it sound so very surprising?'

'I had never thought about it — about you — or me — like that. I thought — I don't know what I thought, except that you were someone I could come running to if anything went wrong.'

'Ah.' He gave a sigh, and a curious little smile. 'In that case,' he said gravely, 'there is not much point in pursuing the matter. I do not want you to bind yourself to me in any way. Neither do I want to embarrass you. And I certainly don't want you to feel you can't come running to me if anything goes wrong. For to whom else could you run, Sarah, except to your dear, foolish mother whom you love so much?'

I still stood silent with astonishment. He laughed and bent his tall head and gently kissed the side of my astounded face. My hand flew to the spot and the colour flamed up in my cheeks. He shook his head and his shrewd eyes were amused.

'No kisses but stage kisses? In spite of all the beaux, the bouquets and the flattery? In spite of being the toast of the town, and the supposedly corrupt ways of the theatre people, this is the first time you have been kissed, isn't it? Well, perhaps it is too soon, and you are too young to think of being a wife.'

We started to walk on again, and I burst out, my eyes full of tears, 'But you would not want a wife like me! You would want a grand wife, who could talk to judges, and give dinner-parties for important men, someone very tall and dignified, and . . .'

'Hush,' he said, 'I don't want anything of the sort, although I am quite sure you could manage all that quite easily if you set your mind to it. You can act the fine lady as you can act the little innocent or the minx. In fact, without any acting, there is a bit of all three in you.' This was what scared me about Robert — in a short while he seemed to know me better than I knew myself. 'What I have always hoped to find in life is someone I can love and who loves me. It is God's greatest blessing. Well, I know I love you. Not wildly, fiercely, desperately or madly like your beaux will protest, which only means, Sarah, that they want to bed with you but are trying to put it more poetically.'

I was well aware of the humorous twitch of the long, fine lips, but I was a theatre girl, and not shocked. But neither was I going to laugh.

'I — just love you,' he went on, 'as you are. I don't know if you love me. But I do know you are stalking different and more dangerous game, Sarah. Mr. Jonathan Sefton has followed us this far, and has just gone off furiously in the direction of the theatre, evidently convinced by our manner to each other, for he cannot have heard our words, that you have another lover.'

He looked down at my face, and said, 'Ah, Sally, don't look like the kitten who has stolen the cream. He is young, rich, handsome, violent and unscrupulous. Do you care for him?'

I could not meet his eyes. 'I would rather not talk about it. I have not encouraged him.'

'Sarah, you know very well your behaviour is driving him mad. To what point of madness — mad enough to ask you to be his wife?'

'Why not?'

'Is that what you want?'

'Yes,' I flashed fiercely. 'For four years this is what I have dreamed of. To be Lady Sefton one day — or to make him want me enough to marry him or send him to the devil, so that he can tell his fine mother there is one girl in London who can do what she likes with him.'

We walked in silence. My hand on his arm had clenched into a tight, tense knot. He put his other over it, and under the warm and gentle grasp I relaxed. 'Very well,' he said, 'we will not talk about it any more. Remember I am your lawyer, and your friend, and will always be here to help you.'

For a moment I was tempted to give up my schemes and to be everything he wished me to be. But always the memory of what the Seftons had done to me — and now the knowledge of what Jonathan would do to me if he could, possess me and disgrace me for his own lust and vanity — these thoughts came first. But I did not remove my hand — there was infinite comfort in Robert's presence and touch. My dreams of revenge were not quite so vivid as I walked by his side.

'How long before you go on tour?'

'Three weeks. My mother has one more week at the Royalty. Two weeks free — then we go north.'

'Well, I have a house in Surrey. It is only a small place which I bought for quiet weekends, not very large, but spacious grounds, and the Wey runs through it so I have some fishing. If you and Herself would care to avail yourself of it for a short holiday, I would be very happy to entertain you. I have a housekeeper and staff, and if you decide to go, I will advise them of your coming.'

'Would you be down there too?'

'Well, perhaps — for a few days. No more. Would you like me to come?'

'I am always glad to see you Robert.'

'Are you, Sally? I wonder.' His voice was dry but as always when he spoke to me, very kind. 'I wonder what you really think of me. Well, ask your mama and let me know when you would like to visit Riverbend.'

We reached the theatre, and Robert made his precise bow and left me at the stage door. I went up to my dressing-room where my mother had already changed into the flowing robes of the unfortunate Lady MacDuff. There was a great bouquet of red roses in a vase, filling the room with fragrance, and I knew who had sent them. I did not even look at the card.

The pretty boy who played her murdered son sat on my mother's knee, while she gave him sweetmeats. It made me think of the time when I too was only ten, just after my father's death, being petted and spoiled in dressing-rooms playing children and fairies, and looking at his little painted face, wondered if he liked it or hated it as much as I had. But then, poor child, he was born in the stews round the Lane, and had not known the gracious life of Rollers Croft as I had.

I told Herself of Robert's offer of a holiday in the country and she brightened. She had been worried over this affair with Jonathan Sefton. She was oppressed, not knowing what to do and quite unable to control me. The idea of getting away from it all for a short while was very welcome. But even so, when she went down to the stage for her one scene, I thought she looked vague and her eyes overbright behind their painted lashes.

I knew the symptoms only too well, and sure enough when I was alone in the dressing-room I found a bottle of spirits hidden beneath the curtain where the costumes were kept. I put it out in full sight and when she came back she saw it at once, and the tears rose to her eyes, and she sat down before the mirror and buried her face in her hands. In a moment I was kneeling beside her, my arms about her.

'Don't cry, Mama darling. What is it? Tell me what is worrying you?'

'That young Sefton you are playing for a gull, he was here again today and insisted on seeing me.'

'You were careful?' I insisted. 'You did not speak of the relationship?'

'Ah, never. I did not at all. Sure, it's not myself who wants to resume that relationship. Not in any way.'

'What did he want with you?'

'He wanted you, Alannah, as well you know, you wicked girl. For haven't you been driving that boy wild ever since you came to town?'

'He drives himself wild,' I said, rising. 'He cannot bear to be refused. He is a Sefton and thinks he can have anything he sets his heart on. If I lost my heart to him — like half these imbecile girls in the theatre, he would be tired of me in a day. I cannot help it if he is an arrogant fool.'

'Now, Sally, men are men and made of different stuff to us and though I don't like him, I think he is suffering.'

'Good. I hope his lady mother knows about it.'

'Sometimes I cannot understand you.'

'Well, tell me what he said.'

'He said your coldness and indifference were driving him mad. He asked me to tell you that you could have anything you wished. Your own house; your own carriage, accounts at all the London shops, jewels, anything. Marriage he could not offer you, because his family would not allow it, and apart from his allowance, and their generosity in paying his bills, he has no money of his own. He said, as you would not speak to him, he could not tell you this, but to assure you that your future would be safe in his hands.'

I stood, picking one of the red roses to pieces. Until that moment I had almost decided to give up the whole of my mad scheme, but now I was chock full of fury and hatred again.

'So! Lady Sefton would put the dogs on me, and her son thinks he can buy me in the market like a piece of merchandise. I will have them both on their knees before I have done with them.'

'Oh, my darling ... please give up. Don't break my heart.'

56

'Why, Mama, there is no need to break your heart ... What did you tell him?'

'I told him not to be tormenting me, and that you were a virtuous girl, and that nothing I could say would change your mind.'

'You did very well. So the day after tomorrow we will pack up and take two weeks down in Surrey, and leave Jonathan Sefton to cool off. I will let Mr. Thornton know tonight.'

Robert accompanied us to his home that first weekend. Riverbend was not old, having been built in the time when the king was regent for his father, a pleasant white two-storied pavilion, with its main rooms overlooking the fine lawn which sloped gently to the banks of the Wey. On the farther side were dense and beautiful woods.

Robert's housekeeper was pleasant, our rooms simple but comfortable. There were horses in the stable and I rode horseback again along the lanes and fields with Robert, delighted that my childhood skill came back to me so easily. There was a small boat, and we rowed on the river, and Robert fished, and we talked, and sometimes I fell asleep among the cushions, and he would let me sleep, and I would awake and find him sitting, quietly watching me, and I had a marvellous feeling of completeness and peace at opening my eyes, and finding him there.

'You are more tired than you know, Sarah,' he said, and I knew he was right. But it was not the work of the theatre, of learning parts, rehearsing or preparing for my tour that was filling me with unrest. It was the thought of Jonathan Sefton which was exhausting my nerves.

In the evenings Robert and I played cards, or he read aloud to us; twice during that long weekend he invited neighbours to dine, and he asked me to play and sing like the other ladies, and all the time presented me to them as someone whom he valued and honoured greatly. Herself was so happy, the Irish country child she was once coming to the surface, happy all the day long, and all the time looking at me reproachfully, hinting when we were alone that I could have all this and a splendid man for the asking and I chose to throw it all away for an evil dream.

On the Tuesday morning Robert had to return to town. His

groom would drive him in the gig to Epsom and there he would take a coach into London. I went with him, for it was a lovely day, and I would enjoy the drive through the summer fields.

As I bade him goodbye, he asked, 'Have you thought of what I have said to you, Sarah?'

'Yes.'

'Well?'

'I don't know, Robert. I still feel I am not good enough or wise enough.'

I expected him to be angry, perhaps because he was entertaining us so beautifully, and it seemed ungrateful, but he laughed, as though at himself, and said, 'I suppose a dry as dust lawyer is not a great temptation to a young girl.'

'It's not that.'

'What is it then?'

There was a long garden at the back of the inn stable-yard, running out into the fields, and we had wandered there while waiting for the London coach to be hitched up.

'It's that you expect too much of me. You expect me to be good and different, and I'm not like that at all.'

'Oh, Sarah,' he said ruefully, 'I have made myself the guardian of your conscience — there's nothing a young, proud person hates more. I won't any more. Do what you wish, so long as you always think of me as your friend . . .'

'Oh, Robert, my dear, dear Robert,' I cried, 'don't ever stop loving me . . . if you did I think I should really be bad . . .' and I threw my arms round his neck like a silly, impetuous child and with a sound that was half a groan and half a sigh his arms tightened about me, and he kissed me and this time it seemed to me that all the words I had ever learned on the stage, the words that the young lovers thought and said, all came true. When he put me down I was white and shaken, and he stood back and I could see his own lips were trembling.

'I shall always love you, Sarah,' he said, and then from the inn yard the postboy's horn sounded, calling the passengers to take their seats, and the coach clattered out on its way, and I got into the gig with the groom and was trotting back to Riverbend.

The house seemed curiously empty without Robert, although he was such a quiet man. It was as if its spirit had departed. I wandered about restlessly, and would not meet my mother's eyes, knowing that she would once again start telling me that I was a mad girl, and indeed remembering his lips on mine, so short a while ago, I began to believe I was mad, although in what way I did not quite know. I had lived with a set purpose in my mind for a long while, and now, unexpectedly, I was not so sure.

We had dinner alone, the long french windows were open on to a terrace, the lawn and the river; big white moths blundered in and fluttered round the glass candle guards. Afterwards we went into the drawing-room, and presently Herself was nodding in a deep wing chair. It was still very warm, with a misty moonlight that told of rain to come. I wandered out on to the lawn and down to the river. In the woods beyond the owls hooted but the nightingales, their mating time over, were mute and silent.

I turned to go back to the house and stood still, a scream rising to my throat. Jonathan Sefton stood there in the shadow of the trees that flanked the lawn, and as he saw me came striding out to my side.

He stood there towering above me, his handsome face like a devil's, it was so tense with desire. He stood silently, and then caught me in his arms, and began to kiss my face and throat. I was quite helpless but I was not frightened. In fact I experienced an awful and exciting triumph. Although I knew physically he could do what he wanted with me, it was I who had him in my power. I remained still in his arms, not moving, not responding, my heart beating fearfully, and presently he set me down and said, 'Speak to me. Speak to me, Sarah!'

'I have nothing to say to you. Except to ask how you dare follow me down here! And how you dare behave like this.'

'You have treated me like a dog,' he said. 'As no other woman in London would dare. You have not answered my letters, and have returned my gifts unopened. You have acted the pure and innocent young girl as skilfully as you do on the stage. Almost I believed in you. And now I find that all the time you have a clandestine lover, that you creep away down here to be with him. You are false and vicious like all women.'

'I think you are mad. I cannot be false to you because I have promised you nothing.'

'I will kill this man who has made you his mistress.'

'You make a mistake. Mr. Thornton has asked me to marry him. Honourably. I am here with my mother as his guest. It is all the invention of your own black heart — because you wish to humiliate and destroy me, you imagine he is the same.'

I turned my back on him and went towards the house, but he came after me and seized my arm. He made me think of a great cat pouncing.

'Sally Thring,' he said, 'you have made me the laughing stock of the clubs in London, and driven me out of my mind. But if I have wronged you I apologise.'

I bent my head but did not speak. The moment I had waited for was upon me, and I was like a hunter watching for the trap to spring.

'I cannot sleep or rest. I think only of you. I cannot imagine life without you. Will you be my wife?'

The mists seemed to clear, and the moon shone brightly over the quiet garden bleaching the flowers white. Here was my moment of triumph, but somewhere in my heart I was thinking, unhappily, that if Robert were only here this could not have happened, and I wished it were not happening, and that I had not been born at Rollers Croft Hall and never set eyes on my cousin Jonathan. But it *was* happening, as I had planned it through many nights of wakefulness, studying my effects as carefully as any part I had learned for the stage.

'I am honoured,' I said coldly, 'and may I ask what your family think of this match?'

'I have not informed my parents.'

'You do not think they will approve?'

'Not — at first. You can scarcely expect it.' It seemed to me that he and his mother had a genius for driving me on to the headlong and wrong-headed action. The very fact that he had not told my aunt and uncle, and he was ashamed to do so hardened my purpose. But he was pleading with me now and it was what I had longed to hear a Sefton do. 'Sarah, let us be married secretly. I am dependent on my parents for my allowance, and they are very generous. I will take a small house for you somewhere, and later, I will tell them . . .'

I laughed.

'What sort of marriage is this that you offer me? To live in a hole-in-the-corner way because Jonathan Sefton is ashamed to marry an actress?'

'I think you are a devil,' he broke out. 'A beautiful, small, white devil.' He suddenly took me in his arms and forced kisses upon me, and when he set me down, said fiercely, 'Am I so repugnant to you then? Do you hate me — and why do you hate me?'

I was trembling, not with fear. I did not love him, I found his arrogant personality unbearable, but I could not deny he was an overpoweringly attractive man.

'I do not hate you,' I said frankly. 'But I do not love you. If I never saw you again I would not care. Therefore if I am cold-blooded about your offer, you cannot blame me. An actress's life is difficult and insecure. What does this offer you make me mean? You have told my mother that you are penniless without the consent of your family. How do you intend to provide for me — and for my mother, for whom I am responsible? Are we to live on your debts? Or do you propose that I shall be the bread-winner, earning my money on the stage while you hang round the clubs, waiting for your family dole. Mr. Thornton is neither very rich, nor of great family. But he offers me more than you possibly can. Devotion, kindness, a modest but very pleasant life to a man of distinction. You have been bidding for me, Jonathan Sefton. I tell you, you will have to raise the bidding a great deal higher than that. Now, if you please, leave me in peace, or I shall call the manservants and have you put off the grounds.'

I walked back to the house without once turning my head, ablaze with an awful triumph. This was how his mother had once dismissed me, and now it was the turn of her adored and precious son to be scorned and despised.

I went in, shut, locked the windows, called the footman to

close the shutters and draw the curtains. I told him I thought I had heard someone moving in the gardens and he said he would tell the groom to let the yard dogs out. Presently I heard them barking outside. I knew that Jonathan would have gone, but I hoped he was near enough to hear them.

I woke Herself, and poured her tea, sitting very stiff and straight. When I went up to my room and looked at my face in the mirror in the candlelight, I was a burning white, my eyes blazing, my pupils so large that my grey-green eyes looked black. It was a strange brilliant reflection that glared back at me like a young witch.

In bed I was shaken by a terrible storm of weeping. I had won the first match, I was on the first step of the road I had set myself to travel — to be mistress of Rollers Croft, but perversely I wished that it had never happened. That I was not Sarah Sefton, but truly Sally Thring, a young girl of the theatre who had never known any other world.

Robert did not come down again, and I was too pre-occupied and restless to enjoy the rest of my stay at Riverbend. When we arrived back at our rooms in Grays Inn Road we had to get ready at once for my provincial tour.

The weather had broken, and although it was still warm, the skies were grey and weeping. Robert called each week as always but there was a constraint between us which had never been there before. Once, to my surprise, he brought up the subject of my mother's early life, and asked the name of the man who had killed my father.

Mama was down with Mrs. Billings, our landlady, with whom she had struck up a gossipy friendship. Mrs. Billings loved to hear about the theatre great, and I, these days, was so self-absorbed, waiting in a strange suspended way, not having heard or seen anything of Jonathan, and certain in my mind and heart that I *would* hear. I was an absent-minded and dull companion, half-listening, inattentive, so she was glad to get away into the bright neat kitchen for a talk and a cup of tea.

'His name? His name was Danjou. Gerard Danjou. She has not told me much about it. He was a boy in London when she was a young actress; his parents were emigrés, poor and aristocratic. There was no question of a match — they were just a feckless young pair.' I smiled apologetically. 'I do not malign her, but you know what Herself is, and can guess what she was when she was young.'

'Yes,' he said gravely, 'I can. Like Pepys said of Nell Gwyn — a true child of the London streets. Sunny, silly and very pretty. So different from you, Sarah — all you have is the prettiness, and with you it's more than prettiness. It's true beauty. Sometimes pure, sometimes devilish, but true beauty.'

'Are we talking about me or Herself?' I pouted.

'I'm sorry — go on with what you know.'

'It's not a great deal. Apparently after the Restoration in France, they were one of the few families of the old régime who had their lands restored and these lands were all in Martinique, so Gerard went out there for some years, and when his father died, and he came into the family inheritance he came back to England looking for Mama — but by then she was married to my father. He followed her down to Rollers Croft, my father discovered them together — innocently, she says. But Sir Gore had, I knew, a terrible temper and was very jealous.' I thought of Jonathan's fierce hawk's eyes and shivered. 'They fought, and Sir Gore was killed. She helped Gerard to escape to France ... She says one death was enough, and perhaps she was right. She told me about it once. She never speaks about it now. She can't bear it, you know — it is when she remembers that she goes into melancholy, and drinks too much. She reminds me of a frightened child longing for comfort, and that is when I have to love her more to take the fear away.'

His eyes softened. 'It is a strange story,' he said, and added gently: 'Whatever the truth of the matter she did not deserve to be discarded as she was. You have been a great comfort to her, Sarah.'

It was the day before our departure, and our trunks had been sent in advance to Sheffield. We were to go on the stage-coach the next day, and had said our goodbyes at the theatre. I had been asked by Mr. Hodgson to return in the autumn at a higher salary, and to take on some of the more famous parts. He was surprised at my lack of excitement, but already I was no longer thinking in terms of a future on the stage. I had a clause written into my contract that I was free to give notice if I married or had any urgent family business.

'Are you thinking of marrying then, my charmer?' Mr. Hodgson asked coyly, though his little pig's eyes were very anxious.

'What young girl does not think so, Mr. Hodgson?' I replied. 'It does not mean that it will necessarily happen.'

'Ah, you'll be off,' he said dismally. 'Off with one of these young gallants one day, emptying my theatre and leaving me bankrupt.'

The afternoon before our departure was hot, Grays Inn Road dusty with a wind that stirred the dust and straws along the gutters. The sewers smelled and the sky was leaden and the city seemed to be longing for the cleansing of rain.

Herself had taken a hackney to the Royalty, to make a final visit to our dressing-room, to collect some grease-paints and small properties that we had left there, and, I suspect, to have a quiet drink with some of her cronies. I made no protest — I was bad company these days, and I trusted her not to go too far.

I stood, leaning my head against the casement, looking at the street. Robert was away somewhere on business, and had already bade us goodbye. Jonathan had sent no word, and I began to think had abandoned his quest, and did not know whether to be glad or sorry. It was like an open door into a quiet and peaceful garden — I could enter or slam it closed and go once more on my strange quest just as I pleased. I knew I only had to make a sign and he would return, but if I did it would be his triumph not mine.

A carriage drew up outside the house and I recognised it at once — the dark blue panels with the crest on the doors, the coachman and footmen on the box, the fine pair of dappled bays. It was the carriage which had brought Sir Hayden, Felicia and Denby to the door of the house in Farm Street. *Denby* — I had forgotten Denby and his earnest, touching adoration.

The footman descended, and lowered the steps, and to my astonishment it was my Aunt Charlotte, Lady Sefton, who descended. I well remembered the tall, straight-backed figure, and hard, arrogant glance. But she had changed. She was still dressed very richly in an old-fashioned, individual style. A full gathered skirt and close-fitting sleeves heavily trimmed with rare, beautifully laundered lace. Her height and straight back gave her an imposing dignity. She was all in black today with a fine mantilla of heavy white silken lace over her shoulders and hair. But as she stood looking doubtfully up at the house I saw that she seemed much older, her face lined and worn, and that the high-combed hair was now heavily streaked with grey.

She mounted the steps and I heard the bell clang somewhere below stairs. Presently Mrs. Billings knocked, and announced, obviously greatly impressed, 'Lady Sefton wishes to see you, Miss Thring.'

She came in and I stood motionless, waiting, wondering whether she would connect the well-dressed, composed, beautiful young woman I was now, with the wild, passionate, gypsy-looking child in the rough clothes who had pleaded with her and cursed at her four years ago.

A vague expression of recollection passed over her harsh features, but was gone immediately, and I knew I was safe. She had not recognised me.

'Miss Sarah Thring?'

'That is my name.'

'My son Jonathan has asked me to call and make your acquaintance.'

I said nothing to this, and she said wearily, 'May I sit down?'

'Please — I am sorry. I did not mean to be ill-mannered. I confess I am — rather startled by your visit. I sent Mr. Jonathan Sefton away in no uncertain terms and did not think to hear from him again.'

'Why did you send him away?'

'Because, Madame, he offered me nothing but dishonour. He wished to make me his mistress. I can earn my keep myself, without descending to this, and I am not for sale. Or he offered to marry me secretly, without informing you or his father. When I marry I shall expect my husband to be proud of me and not wish to hide me away as if I were a disgrace to his name.'

'I see,' she said, and her eyes glittered dangerously. 'You

play for high stakes, Miss Thring. No...' she put up her hand as I would have answered her indignantly... 'No, I am too tired to fight Jonathan any more. My husband has been very ill — still is. Indeed I can see no end to it. I cannot see a recovery...' She hesitated, seemed lost in her thoughts, and said 'The Seftons all seem to meet violent ends. Sir Hayden was a healthy man two years ago, and now, a throw from his horse and he crawls through the days as though each one would be his last.'

'I am sorry,' I said automatically, but I could never be sorry for her. She was suffering now, and she deserved to suffer.

'Jonathan has asked me to receive you. He wishes to marry you. You realise of course that at first I would not entertain such a match — I had such high hopes of him. But he is a boy who will pull the world about his ears if he cannot have his own way — not like my poor husband. He is like his uncle, Sir Gore, who has been dead these ten years.' I kept silent. She was talking of my father whom she had loved.

'I have two sons — one good and conscientious but delicate — Denby — and Jonathan who is so...' she hesitated, then said with a sigh, 'So splendid, but wilful to a point of madness. A true Sefton. I cannot disguise the fact that he has always been my favourite, and now I cannot fight him any more. I have told him I will receive you.' She looked up at me with dark, hopeless eyes, but still I could not feel sorry for her. I remembered that time when she had threatened to set the dogs on me as though I were a criminal. 'You will not expect me to welcome you with joy or affection or any sentimental nonsense. Neither can you expect me not to hope with all my heart that this — romance —' and what a world of sarcasm she put into that word — 'that this romance will come to nothing. But you seem presentable, and as he says, extremely lovely. I would like you to visit us.'

I bowed my head, not saying a word. I loathed her for her insolence but she was playing into my hands, or so I thought.

'I am returning to Rollers Croft tomorrow. I understand from Jonathan that you are going on a progress and will be at Sheffield. Will it be possible for you to spend a few days with us? It is some thirty miles from our house to Sheffield — I can send a carriage for you. It will be a quiet time, as my husband is so ill we do not entertain.'

'I will be happy to come,' I said.

'Very well.' She rose with the same dignified weariness, as though every movement carried its own weight. 'I would rather, Miss Thring, that you were not accompanied by your mother of whom I have had somewhat dubious reports, but you need have no fears about your situation in my house, I assure you.'

This suited my plans — I did not want any confrontation with Mama and Lady Sefton and, indeed, was nervous in case my mother returned before my aunt had gone. If she did not recognise me she would certainly recognise Mama, the woman who had married the man she herself had loved.

I thanked her, my manner as distant as her own, and moved towards the bell rope to summon Mrs. Billings.

'You understand, Miss Thring, that Jonathan depends entirely on his father for his income — when he marries he will rely on our generosity. This will make no difference to you?'

I shrugged indifferently. What difference could it make when one day everything would be his?

'Perhaps you do care for him?' she said, and smiled indulgently. 'Ah, well, it is not at all surprising, for he is a handsome fellow and can be masterful and charming when he wishes. Most girls sigh for him. His cousin Felicia has always adored him.'

'Cousin?' I began sharply. 'I thought . . . I mean, what cousin is this?'

'She is no real cousin. My adopted girl. To think, Miss Thring, I frowned on the match, because I wanted something better for him. To think that I encouraged this foolish idea of a town house so that my sons could meet the daughters of the great families, and all that happened was that Jonathan hung round the theatre wenches and Denby languished after some imaginary dream of romance . . .' she drew her white lace round her, as though drawing a protection against her own angry, disappointed thoughts. I rang the bell, and she said, 'I will expect you, then, the week after next. I will advise you of the exact date and the time the carriage will call if you will let me have your address in Sheffield.'

I gave her the address of the lodgings we had booked. But when Mrs. Billings opened the door to show her out, I could not resist one little extra barb. 'You can always reach me at the theatre, Madame,' I said. 'Good day to you.'

I went to the window and watched her go — at the carriage window I saw a sad, pretty face, and realised that Felicia Marsden was waiting in the carriage for her. As they drove off I saw mother coming along the road gazing with astonishment as the grand vehicle moved away into the traffic.

She came rushing up the stairs, her hand on her heart, breathless with curiosity.

'And who have you been entertaining behind my back? A duke, sure enough, from the foine equipage.'

'It was Lady Sefton. She has invited me to Rollers Croft. That is to say, she asked the little actress, Sally Thring, not her niece, Miss Sarah Sefton. She has no idea who I am.'

Herself had gone very white.

'Sally,' she whispered, 'don't go. Listen, Alannah, listen to me. Don't go. No good can come of it. That young man will bring destruction to you. Don't go, for the love of God, because that house was never a good or happy one for me. I never should have gone there. I did wrong to go, and I've always regretted it.'

I did not listen. I think now at this stage that these plans of mine had no element of reality. I did not think of myself as Jonathan's wife or of Jonathan as another young human being — only that I could turn back the years and reclaim my heritage as my father's daughter.

CHAPTER FOUR

Not only had my newly acquired London reputation preceded me to Sheffield, but I was remembered for my previous work up in the north. The north-country playgoer is faithful to favourite performers and the audiences welcomed me back like a long-lost daughter — to them I was really Perdita. I am afraid this was all a little irksome to good Mr. MacFarren who had billed a week of heavy tragedies to star in his renowned 'heavy' parts.

The first week I played with MacFarren as Desdemona to his Othello, and although I scored a success and looked very pretty with my long fair hair loose, and in the flowing Renaissance robes, I was not happy in the part. The scheming of Iago and the maddened jealousy of Othello made me think too much of my own situation. I could hear Robert's voice, teasing me drily with a note of warning, 'Desdemona. The young lady who was murdered by her jealous husband.' I remembered Jonathan Sefton's eyes following me through the London streets and drawing-rooms and I remembered too the violent tragedy of my father's death. I told myself this was only a play, that these tragedies did not happen in real life, but I still wished I was playing my familiar charming, light comedy rôles.

On the first night I played Jonathan Sefton presented himself very formally in the green room accompanied by his brother Denby. Jonathan with this high curly head, his spotless cravat, his embroidered waistcoat, and the elegant blue coat made by the king's own tailor, seemed an incredibly mondaine figure in this provincial town which he so obviously despised.

Behind his broad shoulders I saw Denby's fair sensitive face looking at me with a hint of sadness. I had not thought about him since that one brief meeting in Berkeley Square. He looked so much younger than his brother — and so much kinder. Both the young men bowed over my hand and the green room ladies fluttered because, of course, here in the north everyone knew the Seftons as a proud and rich Derbyshire family, which pleased my vanity but did not help my peace of mind.

'I trust, Sarah, that you have no objection to my presence here now that my mother has called upon you and I am formally paying my respects to you.'

Jonathan spoke very stiffly as though he had learned the words by rote and only too obviously hated the whole position. It was as though my resistance was an insult to his manhood and if he had his way he would carry me off by force. 'I hope that at last you will find my behaviour satisfactory.'

If it had not been for those hot, blue angry eyes I would have laughed at him. As it was I decided to be equally formal. I curtsied but did not give him my hand.

'I am gratified by Lady Sefton's kind interest in me,' I lied for I was not in the least gratified. I hated her and wanted to outwit and humiliate both her and this adored and arrogant son of hers. 'You must remember, sir, that you are *only* paying your respects. No decision, one way or another, has been reached on my part. I have as yet given no promise to you — or to anyone.'

He bowed again very correctly although his blue eyes glittered with anger.

'May I present my brother Denby,' he said.

I gave Denby my hand with a frank smile and his face lit with pleasure as he bent over it. He was not the same sort of dominating, virile young man as Jonathan, but there was a quality about him that I much preferred. I suppose, in a way, he was like Robert might have been fifteen years ago, scholarly, sensitive and kind. Except that Robert, for all his lawyer's ways, had a fine physique, and Denby was very fine-drawn. There was something unsubstantial about him, as though too fierce a wind might blow him away.

'Indeed I remember your brother,' I said. 'I hope I find you well, sir.' Neither of us referred to our brief meeting on my first day in London.

'I'm well enough,' said Denby. 'I'm one of those boring

people who are never quite well nor ever really ill. You were wonderful tonight in the play, Miss Sarah. I am sorry I had to leave London and never saw you perform there, but I read every notice and heard of your success.'

'And you sent me flowers too.' I laughed. 'Although they had no name on them, I guessed from whom the white violets came.'

He coloured and laughed. He was so sincere and natural, and so full of enthusiasm that I was touched. Jonathan had never spoken of my work as an actress — indeed he had no understanding of it. He had only wanted to possess the pretty girl whom all fashionable London was talking about and boast about his conquest to his rake-hell friends.

'You really like me in the part?' I asked anxiously. 'I've never done tragedy before . . . I'm not quite sure of myself.'

'Well, I don't like the part,' said Denby — I was conscious that Jonathan, left outside this conversation, was fuming — 'Desdemona is not a part for you. You should always play parts that are all sunshine, joyous and lovely like yourself. Gay, full of laughter. Like Rosalind.'

'I have been offered Rosalind when I return to London,' I began, but Jonathan cut in furiously.

'*If* you return to London, and *if* you are free to be on the stage. You might cut a fine figure in breeches, but I would not care to have my wife display herself so upon the boards with every buck in London ogling her.'

The colour started up Denby's cheeks and he turned angrily on his brother, saying, 'You are coarse as a stableboy, Jon, with no better manners.'

'And you are presumptuous, Den,' said Jonathan furiously. 'You see, Sarah, you have enslaved our little poet too. I did not know he had it in him to pay compliments to a pretty woman.'

There was the bristling sense of quarrel between them. They were so utterly unlike. If Jonathan despised Denby's delicacy it was obvious he envied him his brains.

I disliked Jonathan at that moment as much as I did his mother — I loathed their implicit arrogance as though they had the right to ride roughshod over everyone. And yet physically I was excited and attracted by him, and he knew this, as all such men do. When I was his wife I determined he would give me the respect I deserved.

'I should have said that I shall have the chance of playing Rosalind in London next year. Mr. Hodgson has offered me the part if I wish to take it,' and I met his glance with teasing, sparkling eyes. 'I may very well wish to do so — it depends on how welcome you make me at Rollers Croft, and how kind and pleasant you are to me.'

'I am delighted that my mother has asked you to stay,' said Denby eagerly. 'The last time you were at Rollers Croft, four years ago, it was nearly dark, and we frightened you ... this time we shall make amends, and show you how lovely it is.'

'Indeed,' I replied, 'I know very well how lovely it is. But I shall be very happy to see it again.'

Jonathan came every night to see my performance, but he did not bring Denby again. When I enquired after him he said scornfully that he was fussing, like some old maid, to have everything ready for my arrival.

'He can well leave such things to my mother and the servants even though my father does need so much of my mother's attention.'

'It is very thoughtful of him,' I said.

'But still women's work,' he said indulgently. 'When we are married we shall only come to Derbyshire in the autumn, for the hunting and the shooting. We shall have our own place in London. I want the whole town to see how beautiful my wife is. I am sure we have one thing in common, Sarah. Ambition. I am determined to possess you and you are determined to marry into a good position.'

'There is certainly no love lost between us,' I said wrily.

'When we are married I will teach you all about love, Sarah, and I know you will love me then.' His eyes searched my face with a sombre, calculating look; and the colour burned my cheeks and I could not meet his glance. I knew very well what he meant, I had heard of his exploits in Covent Garden and St. James's. It was not what I thought of as love. When I thought of love Robert Thornton came into my mind, so I did not think of it. I thought of this marriage as something fought for and achieved, not as sharing home, life, table and bed with this powerful boy whom I did not even like.

Mr. MacFarren was very willing to give me a few days' leave of absence to visit Rollers Croft Hall. My tumultuous reception in Sheffield had been a little irksome to his theatrical vanity. He had another actress, more experienced and older, to play the tragic parts. He told me to take a week with the utmost graciousness and announced performances of his thundering, eye-rolling Macbeth complete with brilliant effects of storm and witches' sabbath.

Under all his vanity and pompous display he was a simple and kindly man, and I knew he had an old fondness for my mother. They were both Irish and understood each other well. So I put her under his care while I was away.

'Mr. MacFarren,' I said gravely, 'my mother is not coming with me on this visit, as you know.'

'I do indeed,' he said. 'It would be a terrible thing if you both deserted me. And who would the first and second murderers have to murder at all if my Lady MacDuff was gallivanting off with her daughter?'

'Mr. MacFarren, I am very fond of my mother. May I rely on you to protect her while I am away?'

I knew, although I would not listen to her protests, that she was very worried about this visit. Anything that brought her back her old life at the Hall disturbed and distressed her. The restless nights had returned, the muttering dreams, and the apprehensive doubtful look to her plump and pretty face. She implored me not to go, but my mind was made up. She hated playing in Macbeth too, a notoriously unlucky play in theatrical superstitions, and crossed herself feverishly when the announcements were pasted up outside the theatre. So I appealed to Mr. MacFarren. I did not tell him I wanted him to see she was not lonely and neglected, and that she did not drink too much, or fly off with any company that would make her laugh and divert her from her fears. But he knew very well what I meant.

'Sally, me darling,' he said with a low bow, 'I shall be

delighted to protect and care for Herself and will guard her like a brother while you're away.'

So with my mind at rest upon this score I set out for Rollers Croft once again, but not in a carrier's cart, wrapped in a poor grey shawl. In the beautiful Sefton carriage, sent by Jonathan to fetch me, dressed in one of my pretty London dresses of striped green and white gauze and an artful, artlessly expensive bonnet of pale green straw, trimmed with field flowers and silvery wheat ears which had been made for me in Bond Street. No one would recognise the poor little waif in this successful and assured young actress.

It was August, hot, and the corn high and as the horses toiled up the moorland road towards the Hall it was early evening and a huge August moon like a plate of silver heaved itself up from the heat mist hanging over the Derwent Valley. When we drove into the stone courtyard before the pillared portico I looked out at my old home. Rollers Croft Hall, my true home, which I had come back to claim. It was going to be mine again.

Jonathan, Denby and Felicia Marsden came into the big marble paved entrance hall to meet me. Lady Sefton, I was told, was with her husband who was very unwell.

'My father's back injury grows more and more painful, and it is difficult to find any relief for the pain. My mother and Felicia are with him continually,' said Jonathan.

Felicia stared at me unhappily, some of the colour had gone from her cheeks, perhaps with sick-room nursing, but she was still a pretty young English rose. I remembered the child who had stared so resentfully at me from the back of the big black horse in the orchard that day, four years ago, and the expression and attitude was just the same. This was her kingdom, Jonathan her adored one, and I was an intruder.

'It might have been better,' I said, 'if I had put off my visit to another time?'

'Tomorrow,' said Denby, 'I am taking Sir Hayden to Buxton, to see if the hot springs can help. I am against the journey, but the doctor insists.'

'You will be away, while I am here, then?'

'I am sorry to have to say yes. But please enjoy yourself

while you are here. My mother and Felicia will have more time to amuse you when my father has left, and Jonathan has made many plans.'

I noticed it was always Denby who accompanied his sick father.

I was given a room on the south-east side of the house overlooking the lawns and the paddocks which sloped down towards the Derwent Valley. To the right the flower garden was in full summer bloom and under my window the huge magnolia grandiflora opened white waxen cups of scented sweetness. There was a tap on the door and I was surprised when Mrs. Ridstone came in — I knew from her letters that Ridstone was dead and she was working in the house now but I had not thought she would be looking after me. She was darkly gowned and wore, as usual, a spotless apron, but the cap on her greying hair was edged with lace. She closed the door cautiously, and then came forward to give me a hug.

'Riddy. I didn't expect you. I thought perhaps Gilly would be my maid.'

'Nay, our Gilly married a farmer over to Wirksworth last spring, and I'm in charge of t'upstairs maids. Miss Sarah —' she held me away and looked me up and down. 'Aye, but you're a bonny 'un. Who would have thought! Just a scraggy scrap of nowt last time I saw you. Eh, when I heard you were coming, I didn't know what to think. Her ladyship doesn't know who you really are, then?'

'No. And I don't want her to. To her I'm Mistress Sally Thring the London actress, and that's what I want her to think,' and I added silently: 'For the time being.'

'And you're niver going to wed Mr. Jonathan, like they say?'

I drew in a deep breath.

'Yes,' I said airily, 'I think I well might. Why not, Riddy? It is a good match. He is set on it — and it will bring me back here to the Hall which, after all, is my rightful home.

'Miss Sarah, happen I ought not to say this, but Mr. Jonathan is not a good young man.'

'Riddy, few young men today are good. Perhaps it is for their wives to try and reform them.' But she did not laugh and her faded eyes were still very serious. 'Riddy — don't worry — it is for me to decide, and I know what I'm doing.' I changed the subject abruptly. 'So you're not at the lodge now?'

'Oh, aye, I still have my room and sleep there — it's kept by a widow woman, and it helps her to have me lodge there. It helps me, too — your letters come there, Miss Sarah — you mind how I didn't want folks to know as we were writing. You know you and your mama are niver mentioned here at the Hall? Though Mistress Sally Thring is talked about enough of late. The whole house is buzzing with it. An actress, they say. *Mr. Jon and an actress!* Why his mother was after a duke's daughter for him. Well, anyways, I maid Miss Felicia so I've come to see if you need owt.'

'Well, thank you, Ridstone,' I said. I sat down in the window seat while she unpacked, laid out the dress I chose to wear that night, and brought me hot water to wash in before I changed. While she did so she told me all the news.

'It is a sad house now,' she said. 'Once it was all parties and the like and Sir Hayden was a good, kind man whom everyone liked. Now he's that poorly and no one knows how long he will live. M'Lady has had trouble enough.' She eyed me uneasily, and shrugged. 'Well, she's been grand to me. I've never liked her, but then I was fond of your poor mother with her pretty ways. But m'Lady has had a lapful of sorrow, as they say, with the poor master so ill, and the young ones such a trouble — Mr. Denby on account of his health, and Mr. Jon because of his wild ways. He thinks of nowt but hunting and horses, and grand clothes and his smart London friends ... Eh, I don't know! It seems that girls can only see as far as a handsome face. Our Miss Felicia would follow him barefoot across country, I'm thinking.'

There was another tap at the door and when Mrs. Ridstone opened it Felicia Marsden stood there. She wore a dress of dark grey silk with a high white chemisette frilled round her neck rather like a nun's coif.

I had changed for the evening into a dress of lilac gauze — I loved these thin materials that floated round me, accentuating my pretty figure and studied grace. The dress had full short puffed sleeves and a low-cut neck. I had no jewels so I had pinned a spray of artificial muguet into my hair. I had tried for an effect of fresh virginal youth, but when I looked at Felicia I felt my appearance was too studiedly theatrical, and the spring greenness and bare white neck unsuitable for this sad quiet house.

'I came to see if you have everything you want,' she asked, and I bade her come in, and told Mrs. Ridstone to go. I searched among my things and found a white lace shawl and put it round my shoulders. She watched me do so and said, 'It is a pity to cover your arms and shoulders, they are so beautiful — and Jonathan will appreciate them . . . he only has eyes for beautiful women.'

'Thank you,' I said, although I was not at all sure that she meant a compliment. 'Then he will notice you too. You are very pretty.'

'There is no need for you to pretend to be nice to me,' she said childishly, and her round blue eyes filled with tears, 'I hate you, and I don't care if you know it or not. And Jon never notices me. If I walked into the drawing-room naked I don't think he would turn his head.'

I laughed and said I was sure he would.

'You don't know how cruel he can be — or how wonderful too; he can't help it. All the women fall in love with him. That is why he wants you, because you don't really care.'

'You seem to have learned a great deal about me.'

'There has been a great deal of talk about you in this house, I can tell you.' She looked at me and to my horror she was crying. The round blue eyes filled with great tears and ran down her cheeks, 'You won't give him up, will you? You will marry him?'

I was astonished. 'But why should you want me to?'

'Because if you don't I don't know what he might do. He is capable of anything — of killing himself — or you.'

I felt a chill of horror, but did not really believe her.

'But you don't care what happens to me?'

'I should care if Johnny was hanged for murder.'

'How morbid you are.'

'Well, he has gone to such lengths to get you. He talks to me, sometimes — in a funny way. As though I were a boy, or just a sort of listening post. He said he had wagered all his friends that he would have you, and then when you hated him — she looks at me with those cold mermaid's eyes as though she hates me, he said — he began to want you more than anything in the world. It is a humiliation that he should be a laughing stock before his friends, and have to plead with his parents to receive a play-actress. A nobody ... He has brought you to his home now, and asked you to be his wife. If you refused now, it would be terrible. Even his mother is afraid of his temper. She says he is like his uncle who was shot ... not like his father. Denby is like Sir Hayden. I think she was in love with Sir Gore and wanted to marry him — just like me and Jon. But like Jon he fell in love with a worthless actress and brought her here to Rollers Croft, and when his brother and wife would not accept her he threw them out, and would give them no money. I think Jon is like his uncle ...'

I cut in furiously. 'I may be an actress but I am not worthless, Miss Marsden. I have worked and earned my bread and kept myself and my mother in respectability since I was sixteen. I have had no family nor money behind me. What I have done I have done by myself!'

Her soft mouth trembled. 'I'm sorry. I know nothing of such things. It must have been hard for you sometimes.'

'It can be hard, especially if one is not born to it, as I was not.' I stopped, afraid that I had said too much. 'You may have reason to fear me but it is not because I am wanton or a fool.'

She began to mop at her eyes with a fine-edged lace handkerchief. She was a charming, inexperienced, gentle creature.

'I am everyone's fool,' she said tremulously. 'Everyone lectures me. My aunt, my uncle, my cousins, even Ridstone. And now you. It is past bearing.'

I had to smile. 'Poor Cia,' I said. 'At least you expected to look down on a silly, common play-actress. Well, look down on me if you wish, I shan't mind it from you.'

She said, startled, 'You remembered my pet name — from that little meeting in the orchard so long ago.'

'I remember every word of that meeting,' I said. 'You did not tell your aunt about it then?'

'No. We were not supposed to be out so late — it is bad for Denby to go out into the winter evenings. Nor were we allowed to take the black mare out of the stable. It was one of our adventures that we never told her about.'

I sighed with relief because I had no doubt that if they had not told about the encounter in the orchard, Lady Sefton had not mentioned the rough, skinny child she had turned from the door. Indeed she had told me that she never spoke my mother's name or mine since Sir Gore's death. My secret was safe for the present and only the present mattered. When I was Lady Sefton, then I would tell them who I was with a great deal of pleasure.

'Well,' I said, 'let us be friends. It will make the time pass more pleasantly.'

We had really crossed some strange line of friendship. Perhaps because we were girls, and young, with our heads full of dreams — although I would wager Felicia's dreams were more innocent than mine.

My aunt came briefly to greet me; it was obvious that she was deeply concerned with Sir Hayden, and she was preoccupied and a little distraught, anxious about the long journey over the moors which he had to make the next day. While she was there the conversation was necessarily subdued, but after dinner she went back to her husband, and we went to the drawing-room where Felicia was to pour the tea.

But Jonathan did not take tea, he called for some more wine, and asked me if I would like to see the house. But knowing that he wished to get me alone, I said I would if we could all go, which we did, a solemn candle-lit progress through the big rooms, looking at family portraits, old treasures and historic memories of early Seftons. They all looked strange to me, these portraits. I could not relate myself to any of them. Except one — hidden away, unlit in a dark corner — the pretty rosy portrait of my mother as Perdita, ribbons and striped satin, and lace and powdered curls, and fluffy lambs.

'That is the wench my Uncle Gore married,' said Jonathan,

his eyes burning in the candlelight. 'He too was a fool about an actress.'

Denby flushed angrily and I thought for a moment they would quarrel, but after a few minutes' wrangling Jonathan, sick of our formality and their presence and bored with the house which he knew so well, strode off out of the room, banging the door behind him. I looked questioningly at the other two.

'Oh, now he is cross,' cried Felicia.

'And what will he do when he is cross?' I asked.

'Saddle a horse and ride over the moors or go to an inn and drink,' said Denby coldly.

'I am so frightened when he rides like that in the dark. The moors are treacherous — he could fall and be injured like Sir Hayden,' said Felicia.

'It is a brilliant moonlight — Jon rides magnificently and has the devil's luck,' said Denby, and there was a touch of envy in his voice. 'Nothing can happen to him, he is too strong. But as it is so warm, shall we go into the garden. I don't think even my mother will imagine I can catch my death of cold on a night like this.'

So we went down the great staircase and out across the terrace into the gardens. Felicia had called her fluffy little dog to come with us, and ran ahead with it, leaving Denby and me behind.

'As you have decided to marry Jon,' he said to me, 'I can only wish you every happiness. Be sure I will do everything I can to help, and to persuade my parents to settle a comfortable income on you.'

'I have not decided yet,' I said.

He stopped, and took my hands.

'Sarah,' he said, 'I cannot hope that you can care for me. I know, compared with Jon, I have little to attract a beautiful girl. I am not strong and handsome, and because I must care for and spend time with my father I have little time. And because of my wretched health my mother has kept me from the world in some ways. She was always anxious unless she had care of me — I was never away from home until I went to university.

So far as the world and women are concerned, Jonathan has had all the adventures, and I know many women love him. But — since you have told me you are not yet committed to him — I feel free to tell you how much I love you.'

'Why, Denby,' I said gently, 'you do not know me.'

'It does not matter. Ever since that first meeting, when Jon frightened you so, and you lay against my shoulder, so thin and pale and small with your lovely hair all about you, I have dreamed of you. At Oxford, when I read for my degree, you were all the magic girls of history and poetry to me, Beatrice, Rosalind, Sabrina . . . the elf girls of Celtic legend . . . whatever I read — they all bore your face. And now you are older, and even more beautiful. I want you to know, whatever happens, how much I love you . . . and if ever you should come to care for me, or not even that — if you should just want the protection of my name and home, I should be most proud to make you my wife.'

Absurdly, I burst into tears. I was not acting at all. I was desperately touched by his sincerity and his innocent worship. He was older than I was by nearly three years, and yet he seemed to me to be the merest boy compared with either Robert or Jonathan. And so vulnerable. I could have hurt him with a word or just as easily I could have made him blissfully happy.

'Why are you crying? Have I made you unhappy?'

'No, Denby, you have made me happy — because you are so good. I am very honoured that you love me, but I think you could find a better girl than myself.'

'No, I could not,' he said earnestly, 'because there is no other girl in all the world for me.'

Felicia came running back with her little dog. The gardens were drenched in moonlight, and the scent of stocks and lavender filled the air. The house, its dark bulk against the sky and its windows glittering in the moonlight, looked very beautiful. But I felt a confused stranger there now — I did not feel, as I had expected to feel, that I had really come home.

Presently I bade them good night and went to my room. Ridstone came up to light the candles, and lay out my night clothes. I bade her good night and went to bed but could not sleep. It must have been in the early hours of the morning when I heard a horse galloping furiously towards the house, and guessed Jonathan had come home. I rose, made no light, crept to the window, and looked out — the moon was setting and the first grey light of dawn was in the sky. I saw him come round the house, with his striding, panther-like walk, and stop below. He threw his head back, his face towards the sky, his eyes fixed on my window. I did not move. I was afraid. In one hand he clenched a riding-whip, and his whole magnificent body was tense as though every muscle was knotted with anger. It was as though he would beat me into submission if he could. He stood there, motionless for several minutes, and then turned away and went round to the entrance of the house.

I stayed awake, listening, and I heard him come up the stairs and along the corridor and pause by my room. I heard him knock, very gently, I heard his voice say, agonised, 'Sarah . . . Sarah . . .' and I rose, put my wrap about me, and opened the door.

A shaft of moonlight fell through the high window on the stairs, lighting his tall figure. I could see he was trembling.

'Sarah,' he said, 'if I have offended you I am sorry — but I am beside myself with thinking about you. I cannot stand this uncertainty. I have been a crazy fool, I know, but now I cannot deny that I have never known what it was to love, to desire, to worship a woman before. I have done everything I can — tell me now that you will be my wife.'

I had won. Whatever I felt for him I knew now I could have all the things I had always dreamed of having. I put out my hand and he seized it, and held it against his lips.

'Yes,' I said, 'I will marry you, Jonathan.'

He bent his head over my hand. I felt tears wet against my fingers, and was frightened that this strong, passionate young man could be so shaken. I drew back, took my hand away, saying, 'You must go. In the morning we will talk . . .'

'Oh, Sarah, Sally . . . my darling . . .'

'Good night.'

I closed the door, slid home the bolts. I heard him go away, and then fled to my bed. Sitting there in the moonlight my triumph slowly died, and I said aloud in the big silent room, 'What have I done? What have I done? Robert, my dearest friend... what have I done...?'

I slept uncertainly and rose early in the morning. I looked out of my window at the ground, the gardens and paddocks in the morning light, and my courage and purpose came back. It was a prize worth winning. Before Mrs. Ridstone brought my hot water I wrote to Robert. I told him what had happened. I had wanted to marry Jonathan and be Lady Sefton and now I was going to do this. It was a great match, it would restore me to the life I had been born into, and it had been for many years my heart's desire. I signed the letter, addressed it and gave it to Mrs. Ridstone to post. What I really longed to do was to ask Robert to come to me at once and take me away, because although I was borne up with the triumph of my conquest, somewhere within me I was uncertain and terribly afraid.

Early that day Denby left with his father for Buxton. Sir Hayden was wheeled out by two footmen and I was startled to see how terribly ill he was now. His face, so uncannily like Denby's, was racked with pain and shrunken to an unearthly thinness. Denby walked close to him, holding his father's hand, and I saw him wince silently as Sir Hayden's grip tightened at every jolt.

Lady Sefton, with the nurse and doctor, went ahead to the carriage, arranging about rugs and pillows, a case of light food, a flask of brandy, and containers of water to be put inside. She was travelling to Buxton with Denby and his father, but would return that same day.

I had breakfasted in my room — I had wanted to put off my meeting with Jonathan as long as possible. I was committed now, and did not want to face the fact. The day had dawned uncomfortably hot — even the moorland wind seemed to have failed. The chestnut trees stood with slack motionless dusty leaves, and when dawn broke lightning had flickered along the horizon. Jonathan had met me with a brief word and kissed my hand, and as they brought Sir Hayden out into the hall, he drew my hand through his arm. I saw Felicia's eyes fill with tears, and that she pressed her hand to her lips to stop crying. Denby glanced at me once, but said nothing. Lady Sefton was too occupied and too anxious to notice.

Jonathan had told me that because his father suffered a great deal of pain he took regular doses of laudanum, and I thought that this morning he must already have been given some to help him on the long drive over the moors.

Jonathan led me forward and, as I curtsied, he said, 'Father, this is Miss Sarah Thring who has consented to be my wife.'

Sir Hayden looked up at me in a vague, bemused way, signalling to the footmen to halt his wheel-chair. He appeared to know me, gazing at me earnestly, and then said vaguely, 'Molly ...' I shivered, for he was living in the past, mistaking me for my mother.

'The pretty girl,' he said vaguely, 'the pretty actress come to ruin all our lives. To set brother against brother. Poor child, poor child. Such a foolish innocent. She was not to blame — it was evil passions that were to blame. Jealousy. A terrible thing jealousy. I told Charlotte she must not say those things to Gore, but she would not listen. He never spoke to us ... not to either of us again ... and then I heard he was dead ... shot ... jealousy, always jealousy ...'

'He is wandering,' said Jonathan stiffly.

'Come, Father,' said Denby. 'Mother is waiting at the carriage.'

The men pushed the chair across the great entrance hall with its floor paved with black and white squares of marble, then carried it down the steps and lifted Sir Hayden out of it bodily and into the carriage. I heard him cry out with pain before they settled him among the pillows on the seat.

I went out on to the terrace. I knew he had been speaking about my mother — that in his confused and drugged mind I was my mother, Molly O'Brien, the little Irish flirt, who had so thoughtlessly brought such tragedy to his family — and it was strangely ominous that he should mistake me for her at such a time. I was grateful that Lady Sefton had not been within hearing.

After they had gone Jonathan and I spent most of the day riding — I loved this exercise and so did he: indeed it was one of the very few things we had in common. I insisted, though, that Felicia should accompany us and he laughed when I said demurely that it would not be proper for us to spend the day alone together.

'I shall not press you, Sally. You are mine now and I can afford to wait a little while longer to have you quite alone.'

It was early in the afternoon when a man came riding in with a message for Jonathan. Sir Hayden had reached Buxton only to die as they carried him into the rooms they had taken near the spa. His mother had written hurriedly, obviously distraught, telling him to come to her and Denby as soon as possible.

He was ready within the half hour. He bade Felicia and me goodbye, and looked deeply into my eyes. For a moment I thought he would kiss me, but he only bent over my hand.

'This may delay our plans a little,' he said, 'but I shall soon be back. I must get you a betrothal ring — not up here — in London. The finest I can find. Wait here until I return.'

He swung up on to the strong, sturdy cob and trotted off along the drive. Felicia and I turned to each other.

'I suppose,' I said, 'he is Sir Jonathan now.'

'Oh, no,' said Felicia, 'Denby is the heir. They are twins but Denby is the elder by an hour. It has always been a great distress to Lady Sefton that Jonathan is not the heir. He is so much stronger and so much more suited to running a great estate. But it is strange that people so often take it for granted that he is the eldest — he looks so much older I grant you. But it is not so.' She looked at me in concern. 'But surely you knew this?'

'I did not know.'

'But it will make no difference to your feelings for Jonathan? I do not think he could bear to lose you now. I think it would drive him mad.'

I had no feelings for him — only an uneasy fear and the elementary stir of physical response at his touch. I had promised to marry a man I did not love and never could love. For what? A child's stupid dreams of conquest and revenge. A worthless, selfish but passionate pride.

Suddenly in that house of mourning I began to laugh and Felicia and the servants looked at me with shocked faces as though I had suddenly gone out of my mind.

CHAPTER FIVE

I ran away.

I lost my nerve and my head and could think of nothing else to do. I still wonder to the end of my life if Sir Hayden had not died, and I had not learned that Jonathan was the younger brother, whether I would have carried through with the marriage. I think not. I hope not. I think that I had not considered the reality of such a marriage, and I would have realised this before my wedding day. But that day I just bolted like a silly, scared mare, back to my mother, the theatre, and the familiar things of life.

I could not face Jonathan's return from Buxton and tell him I could not marry him and ask him to release me, although that would have been the brave and wise thing to do. But at twenty, when one has played with fire and been badly burned, one is not always wise.

I only took Mrs. Ridstone into my confidence — she seemed as scared as I was, although she considered it the right thing to do.

'Aye, he'll tear t'place apart,' she muttered as she packed for me. 'He can be a terrible young man when he's crossed. You watch out, Miss Sarah, when you get back and don't let him near you alone until he's cooled off. Aye, but you always were a stubborn bairn, and you're no better today.'

She sent a message to the stables and ordered a carriage to take me back to Sheffield. I sat down and wrote to Jonathan.

I told him quite bluntly that I had changed my mind. I told him I was quite aware that I had been unforgivably selfish, wicked and wrong-headed, but then we had both been that. We had both wanted each other for the wrong reasons, and neither of us, in all honesty, had been deceived. I had wanted to be Lady Sefton and he had wanted to impose his will on me. I said I was going back to take up my career in the theatre and I begged him not to follow me or attempt to make me change my mind. That I hoped he would not be angry, that he would remember his mother's sorrow and be a comfort to her and to forget me. I said I knew his mother would be happy to know the marriage would not take place for she had not liked me and had higher ambitions for him. I was deeply sorry. I could say no more. I signed it Sally Thring, sealed and addressed it and went to find Felicia. I felt as though I had escaped from some evil of my own contriving and had been granted a second chance.

It was by now mid-morning and in spite of Sir Hayden's sudden death the great house went on with its functions like a village, servants, gardeners, stablemen all about their tasks, and today all of these were working for the sole benefit of one young girl, Felicia, for I was leaving at once and would not even stay to take a midday meal with her.

I found her on the terrace in the shade of a great cedar tree which spread the wings of its dark branches across the paving stones. She had changed into her dark grey silk and wore black ribbons round her waist and in her hair.

She looked up when I came towards her. Her needlework and books were beside her on the seat, and the little woolly dog lay panting at her feet, too hot for its usual games. I was wearing a light dress of sprigged muslin, and a simple straw bonnet.

'Why, Sarah,' she protested, 'should you not find some kind of mourning? I am sure you can find a dark dress that would be more suitable.'

'Cia, I am leaving now. I think it best. I have no place in this house of mourning and I think it is better that I should go before any of the family return from Buxton. Will you give this letter to Jonathan for me?'

She took the letter, and went white, looking at me fearfully. 'You have decided not to marry Jon?'

'Yes.'

'Because he is not the owner and Denby will get the title?'

'Yes,' I said uncompromisingly.

She said coldly, 'Why don't you stay? It is obvious to anyone that Denby is as mad for you as Jonathan. You could easily marry him if you wish, although Jon will probably kill you both if you do.'

It was my turn to feel the colour fade and my heart stir uncomfortably in my breast. It was Jon's anger I was afraid of. But I said firmly, 'I have decided I do not wish to be Lady Sefton after all. It seems to me the price is too high. I am going back to the world I know, where at least my future depends upon my own efforts. I think it is more tactful to go now — while everyone is away. I think they will all be glad — Jon too, when he thinks about it. You should be glad, Cia . . . have you ever thought it is your own fault that he has never noticed you? Perhaps if you encouraged Denby, or some other young man, he would see how pretty you are.'

'I *couldn't* do such a thing.' She was shocked.

I looked into the round and innocent blue eyes, and said reluctantly, 'It might have been better if I had not. But please give him the letter.'

'I will see he gets it — I dare not give it to him.'

'Just as you wish. I am going now, for the chaise is waiting for me. Goodbye, Felicia . . . try and be happy.'

As I walked back she came running after me, pushing her hand pleadingly through my arm.

'Sarah, I know you don't really believe me when I talk about Jon, but do take care. When he knows you no longer wish to marry him, I am sure he will come looking for you. It is not that he is really cruel — but when he cannot get what he wants he seems to break — I cannot explain. When we were children I always knew he wanted to be his father's heir. And his parents wanted it too, for he was strong, and so much more suited in every way to look after a country property and a great fortune. I don't think he realised until he was a boy of ten or so that by law everything would go to Denby, that he must rely on his parents' good will for anything he received. He became impossible, teasing and tormenting poor Den, defying his parents and behaving badly... even at school it was because he was a great fighter, and so handsome, and a sportsman that he was popular ... at university he mixed with all the wealthy dissolute young men ... as though because he couldn't be the heir he would pull the family down with him. He — he does seem to have changed since he thought you might marry him ... but when he learns that you will not, I cannot think what he might do. You will take care?'

I promised her — she had succeeded in frightening me a little. And I remembered the old tragedy of my own father.

The coachman was waiting with a light chaise into which he had already packed my luggage. As we topped the slope in the drive, I looked back at the house standing in its uncompromising stone solidity under the blazing August sun. Across the fields I could hear the voices of the farm-workers getting the harvest in, and the ditches were high with meadow-sweet and scarlet patches of poppies. Like blood, I thought. I shuddered and turned away from the house which I had so longed to possess, not caring whether I ever saw it again.

The light chaise bowled along the road to Sheffield. I must not be fanciful. It was only in plays that people did dreadful and frightening things. People were law-abiding and young men no longer fought duels and carried pistols. Now I had decided on the right course — the course that Robert had implored me to take, I had nothing to fear.

I told myself that Jonathan would be angry, humiliated by being jilted by someone he thought of as a chit of an actress, but it did not comfort me. I knew he was like me, there was tenacity in him that would not let him give up anything he had set his heart on, even if it were wrong.

As we crossed the Derwent I was thinking anxiously. I could leave Sheffield — indeed I could leave the country because Mr. MacFarren had had offers from Ireland and also to take a company across the Atlantic to America where European artists were beginning to travel to be fêted and highly paid in the big cities of the new Union. I was being ridiculous. I had not committed any crime that I should think of fleeing the country — I had simply changed my mind.

We went slowly, because the driver did not want to force the horses in that blazing heat. Today I had thrown ten years of dreaming away. Dreams I had hugged to me and nourished since the day my father had been killed. To be reinstated, to be a lady again, rich and protected. Dreams that had filled my days ever since my aunt, Lady Sefton, had sent me from the house like a thieving gypsy or beggar, to put myself in her place, to wield her power and humiliate her as she had once so cruelly humiliated me.

I needed new dreams from now on, and they must be based on reality — I could work, as I had worked for the past years, make myself the best in my profession, earn money and fame, travel perhaps across far seas, learn different languages so that I could play in other countries — I could care for my mother and make her life easier, and perhaps set up a home for us together where we could live in peace.

But this was not what I really wanted, and as the hours went by I had to face this fact more clearly. What I wanted at the moment was Robert Thornton, the man who had caught my respect from our first meeting and now had all my love. I thought of the cold, boasting letter I had written to him, and the tears began to run down my face. I wondered if he would answer my letter, and hoped he would not — and yet feared he would not, and yet hoped again he would, so that I could write again and tell him it was all over, and that I knew now how wrong and foolish it had all been.

It was late in the afternoon when we came in sight of Sheffield, its foundaries, mills and innumerable dwellings all belching smoke into the air, which on this hot, airless day hung like a pall in the bowl surrounded by green hills and climbing moorlands. Lit by the rays of the brassy sun it was more theatrical than the stagiest stage set that Mr. MacFarren could have devised.

Mama and I had taken lodgings in a pleasant stone-built house a little way out of the town, in the picturesque country towards Wharncliffe. When the gig stopped, I got down and my mother came flying down to greet me.

'Whatever has happened, Sally darling? I had thought you were staying some days.'

'Sir Hayden died yesterday.'

'Ah, the poor man.' She crossed herself. 'God rest his soul.'

'And I have decided, Mama, that you were right and I was quite wrong. I am not going to marry Jonathan. I do not wish to be Lady Sefton or to live at the Hall. From now on I am going to be Sally Thring and try to be the best comedy actress in England.'

To the surprise of the coachman who had been carrying in my luggage she sat down on the bottom steps and burst into tears of sheer relief.

I sat down beside her and hugged her, and she hugged me, and I cried a little too.

'Oh, Sally, my darling, if you knew what a relief it is to me to know you are not going on with this mad idea. Nothing but bad could have come of it. And what have we to do at all with gentry, when we're doing so well, and in such comfort now? Holy saints be blessed, we can do without Seftons and always could, and I was a fool myself to ever get ideas above my station.'

I laughed at her relief — it was so extraordinarily intense. As though a great load had been lifted from her. I had not seen her look like that in years.

She mopped her eyes, and told me Mr. MacFarren was upstairs in our parlour, that he had come for a dish of tea, God be praised, and had been hoping I would return, for though of course he would never admit it, men being such vain creatures, the Macbeth had not gone down too well, and the good people of Sheffield had wanted to see me again.

'Sure, you're a great little favourite here,' she said as we went upstairs. 'And would you believe it, Himself — ' she thumbed an expressive gesture to the closed parlour door — 'is talking seriously about a season in America, and you and I to come with'm, if we are not terrified out of our wits at crossing the ocean.'

She opened the door, and Mr. MacFarren rose to greet me. The table was laid with one of those substantial West Riding meals of cold meats, home-made breads, pasties, cakes and tea, and there was a bottle of port on the table.

He took my hands, and bent over them in the courtly manner he had acquired through playing kings and great lords, and said he was delighted to see me.

'I am truly delighted, Sally, that you should have decided to return. Not that you wouldn't have graced the aristocracy, but you will grace the boards of the theatres of the world a great deal more. I will have the bills put out tonight that we will play *The School for Scandal* — next week — and I shall play Sir Peter and you shall play my lady.'

We filled the glasses ceremoniously and we toasted the success of the next production.

I asked my mother if any letters had come for me, but she told me there was nothing for me and I managed not to look disappointed. Robert had not written, and there was no reason why he should. Perhaps he would not concern himself with me again.

But my longing to be back at Rollers Croft had gone for ever. I was freed at last of that obsession. My mother's blarneying ways and dear Mr. MacFarren's grandiose posturings no longer irritated me — indeed, they seemed unutterably funny and sweet. We were players and these were the manners of players, and these people whom I had looked down upon welcomed me without criticism and loved me generously.

I pulled off my expensive bonnet and threw it up to the ceiling, and imitating my mother, shouted, 'The holy saints bless us for I was niver so glad to be back anywhere in all me loife!' And we all burst out laughing.

The oppressive heat continued. The streets in the centre of the town, filled with heavy drays pulled by horse teams dragging goods along the roads and wagon-ways to be loaded on the canal barges or to the main goods yards in Rotherham, were dusty and dirty, and loud with the crack of whips and shouting of the draymen. All the talk among the business folk was about the railways that would soon be built to take their coal and steel quickly to the ports.

But we lived outside the town and drove into the theatre in a hired hackney so our lives were not unpleasant, and during those days, before the Sefton brothers came back so disastrously into my life I was at peace even if I was not really happy. I worked hard at rehearsals, I was on better terms with the company whom I saw now as colleagues and not with the superior eyes of Miss Sarah Sefton. And in the afternoons when I did not work Mr. MacFarren, Herself and I drove out to the crags, becks and beautiful moorlands towards Penistone.

And then I took my courage in my hand and wrote to Robert again, a very different kind of letter from the last, and one I found very difficult to write. I cannot tell how many pages were written and destroyed before it was finally finished. I had never for a moment doubted the sincerity of his love for me. I told him simply of the mistake I had made, and how I realised how wrong I had been. I had given up all my schemes and plans to achieve my revenge on Lady Sefton and rule Rollers Croft Hall as its mistress. I said I knew my treatment of Jonathan had been despicable. I said I hoped Robert would understand and forgive me, and I was longing to see him again. I did not say I prayed and hoped he would still love me and ask me once again to be his wife. I sealed this letter, addressed it to Robert, and took it to the mail office myself.

But the days passed and no answer came, and my edgy pride revived. However often I told myself that Robert had always forgiven me, and was the only person who knew all about my pride and vanity, and my ruthless ambition, but still loved me and found something good behind all my pretences, I still could not bring myself to write again.

As every mail coach came into the inn I sent a messenger, or went myself to meet it, but there was no letter, and Robert did not come. The out-of-school feeling of freedom with which I had fled from Rollers Croft began to go, the dusty, murky industrial town beneath the oppressive heat began to weigh on me. If I was reconciled to my work and position, I knew I would never be reconciled to losing Robert Thornton, I knew how how much he meant to me.

I began to think seriously of Mr. MacFarren's offer of an American tour. I will not deny that there was a touch of theatre as well as childishness in my unhappiness, but beneath everything there was a real and desolate sense of loss.

I wondered if Robert, being away from me for these past weeks, had thought differently of the whole matter. He was some years older than myself, not an infatuated boy like Denby or a determined rake like Jonathan. He was a grave and clever man of business — he had said, very simply and tenderly, that he loved me, but now — had he changed his mind? If he did not think I was worth his love I would rather not meet him again. If I left the country for America perhaps I could stay there and build a completely new life.

One night, after we had opened in *The School for Scandal* I arrived at the theatre and as I opened the door of my dressing-room the scene of a summer garden wafted out to me. The whole room seemed filled with flowers.

Behind me Herself said in awe, 'The saints preserve us, it's like Holy Church on Easter morning. Whoever is it that's after you this time, Sally?'

My dresser was beaming. She was a London girl who had travelled up with me and missed the sophistications of Drury Lane. She found the local beaux lacking in style for all their money. This was the sort of thing she expected for a popular leading lady.

'The young gentleman who ordered them is waiting to see you in the green room, Miss Sally. It is Sir Denby Sefton.'

I looked at my mother and saw the pleasure in her eyes fade to dismay. She thought I had put the Seftons behind me for ever — and so had I.

'Oh, no,' she said. 'Tell him to go, Alannah.'

'But I must see him,' I said, 'It's the only way.' I took her arm. 'Come with me, darling. I promise I will send him away.'

We went back-stage and through the slip doors into the auditorium and up the steps to the dress circle.

Above our heads and down below the gallery and pit had already begun to fill. The artists' room was in the front of the house and a few of the cast were there, talking to friends. And there, very slim in his mourning, his bright fair hair shining beneath the candlelight, stood Denby. His hands, holding his hat, were tightly clenched, his face pale, his eyes fixed on the door, and as I came in he came straight across to meet me.

'Denby,' I said, but he began to speak impetuously, as though we were alone, and to stop him, I brought my mother forward.

He bowed with his easy, boyish grace — he looked so very young although he was two years older than myself.

'I am sorry about your father,' I said. 'I hope your mother is well.'

'Thank you — she is as well as to be expected, but . . .'

'Denby. I am sorry too that I left so precipitately. But I thought it for the best.'

'Yes, indeed. Sarah, I have scarcely been able to wait until these last few days have passed. I know it may appear to be an unseemly haste after my father's death — but I was so afraid the company would move on, and I should be unable to speak to you. And speak to you I must . . .'

'Denby, I cannot think what you should want so urgently with me . . .' I was falling into my old ways of feminine prevarication — I knew very well why he was here, and his reproachful eyes confirmed this. 'Denby.' I spoke in a low voice. 'We cannot talk here . . . People can hear. Whatever is said between us will be all over the town tomorrow.'

'I am staying in the town,' he said. 'I have rooms at the Falcon Inn — will you and your mother do me the honour of taking supper with me tonight after the performance? Please, Sarah, I shall be so happy if you will. You know that there is no need for you to fear or run away from me — whatever you decide to do now or in the future.'

I stopped him again. I could see that there would be an impetuous declaration of his feelings for me before the company present, who were already looking and listening, as well they might. I felt very guilty. I was fond of Denby — in the brief time I had known him he had endeared himself to me, his direct simplicity and gentle, boyish sincerity were in such contrast to Jon's passionate wilfulness. I did not want to hurt him in any way. But I must stop this before I became involved.

'Dear Denby,' I said, 'I do not think it would be wise for me to take supper with you after all that has happened. But after the performance my mother and I will call on you at the hotel, and we will talk for a little. Thank you for the flowers — you must have robbed every glasshouse at Rollers Croft. I will see you later at your hotel.'

We went back to my dressing-room and I made up and put on my elegant London dress of striped pink and white satin and plumed turban to play the fashionable ninny, Lady Teazle. It had been one of my favourite parts, but tonight although I did my best, and the laughter appeared to flow, and applause followed my every exit I was in no mood for the acid-tongued wit of this comedy. I was full of apprehension. I could see Denby sitting in the stage box, his eyes fixed on me, applauding my every entrance and exit. The heat in the house was unbearable and the smell of oranges from the gallery and pit overpowering.

The theatre emptied quickly at the final curtain as the audience sought the cooler air of the streets and I hurried back to my dressing-room. As I greased off my make-up I could see my naturally pale skin was paler than ever, and there were dark shadows about my eyes.

'Don't be going to see this young man,' my mother said pleadingly. 'Don't go, darling. Send the dresser with a note, saying you are not well, for indeed you look like a ghost this evening.'

'I feel I must go, Mother,' I said. 'I seem to have done bad things to the Seftons because they have done bad things to me. I feel it's the Sefton in me that's to blame for everything so far, and it's time I stopped. Denby is not like Jon — he's a gentle soul. I'll wager that I am the first girl he has ever noticed. Indeed he has told me so. I don't want to humiliate him. I will go and tell him the truth — that I do not love and cannot marry him.'

I dressed quickly in a summer muslin, carelessly plaiting and winding my hair, and wrapping a thin shawl of flowered silk about my head and face. I did not wish to be recognised going into the hotel.

There was the usual group of admirers outside the stagedoor. Some of them had gifts of flowers, many were boys and young men who gazed at me with adoration and some with surprise that this pale, fair girl could be the same as the pretty chit they had seen on the stage such a short while ago.

I thanked them mechanically and stepped into the carriage followed by my mother. As I glanced back I saw a tall fellow in black move away to the other side of the road and fear struck through me. The sudden, impatient, catlike movement, the powerful shoulders. I could not see his face but I was sure it was Jonathan — he had stalked me so often through the London streets and drawing-rooms. I cried out in fear and my mother put her arm round me.

'What is it, Sally, what is the matter?'

'Nothing ... nothing ... I just thought ... no matter. Oh, it's the heat and I am overwrought. I shall be glad when this tour is over. We are too near to Rollers Croft. I shall be glad when we move to York and then to Edinburgh, farther away. I have been thinking of this talk of MacFarren's about America ... it might be a good idea. We might even stay there and make great fortunes like some emigrants do ...'

'I've a brother over there in New York City and a stack of cousins,' she said and I knew she was talking for the sake of talking. As though she was afraid of any silence.

'I'd dread the sea voyage, though why I don't know, for whenever I've been to Dublin I've been so sick all the way and back that I haven't cared a ha'porth if the blessed boat sank or not.'

It was the kind of thing she said to make me laugh, but tonight I could not laugh. A hot wind rose and stirred the dust and suddenly lightning flickered across the sky.

The Falcon Inn was the best hotel in the town and only a short distance away from the theatre. When the carriage drew up, Denby was standing at the entrance door, waiting to receive me. He came forward and handed me out of the carriage, and led us into a private dining-room on the first floor. In spite of my decision not to eat with him there was champagne on ice, and fruit and sandwiches laid on the table, and here again, flowers set out as for a royal reception.

'Oh, Denby!' I protested. 'I told you we would not stay.'

'You and Mrs. Thring will take a glass of wine?'

'Yes, but ... we must talk, and briefly, Denby. For I am tired after playing and need to rest ...'

He poured out three glasses. I wondered if he had been drinking, for his cheeks seemed flushed, and his eyes brilliant, but I think it was just excitement. In his delicate way he had great beauty.

He raised his glass and said, 'To Sarah Thring. The most beautiful and the cleverest actress in England. My future bride — the future Lady Sefton.'

I met Herself's terrified eyes, and put my glass down.

'No, Denby,' I said, 'you must not speak like this. I am very fond of you and could be your friend, which I think would have been impossible with Jonathan. But anything else, *no*! I will be going soon. A few more days back to London, and then on. I shall go to York and on to Edinburgh, and then who knows — back to London. Perhaps to America.

'America?' he repeated and his flushed cheeks went white. 'You cannot go so far from me. I should die.'

'No, Denby. You will not. Please believe that I mean what I say.'

'But — I have loved you for so long,' he insisted. 'Not like Jon. I would care for you. You should do exactly as you wished. You can stay on the stage, and use my name if you care to. I shall only be proud of it. I am Sir Denby now, and all the assets in the family are mine to do with exactly as I please. Anything you want and I can get for you, you shall have.'

'Dear Denby,' I said, 'no. There are many sweeter and kinder girls who will love you. Your mother would only want me under sufferance. She would only have tolerated me as Jon's wife. I do not want to be married under such conditions. I do not care for you like that, and if you must know I care deeply for someone else — not Jon, someone quite different.'

'You are going to marry him?'

'I do not think so now. But — do not want to marry anyone else. So you must let me go, and not be unhappy ...' I went up to him, and because I was so sorry for him, and so fond of him, and perhaps because I was so much an actress that I could not resist rounding off the scene, I put my hands on his shoulders and kissed him in farewell, and it was at that moment that Jonathan Sefton came bursting into the room.

I hardly know what happened. I know that Herself screamed and rushed forward, and was thrown aside like a rag doll by one movement of his arm. I knew Jon was drunk in some terrible cold, automatic way — perhaps with hatred rather than drink. He took Denby's collar between his hands and shook him like a rat, and then threw him aside, and then turned on me.

I shall never remember his exact words. It was a torrent of abuse, and beneath the foul names there was this terrible underlying current of truth — or what had until his father's death been the truth about me.

He called me a whore and harlot. He said I had driven him mad and then cast him aside, that Felicia had told him I had thought that he was the heir.

'So you turn to that milk-sop, that puny, delicate creature, you insult me by preferring him.' He stopped, drawing great breaths as though he was choking, pulled at his cravat with his left hand. His right was hidden behind him. 'Sarah,' he implored, 'Sarah — even now, even now, I will forgive you anything if you will come back to me. I will not be poor, not as rich as Master Lily-white there, but not poor ... and maybe one day I will have my father's title. The doctors do not give great hopes for his life and I give no hopes for any brats he might produce ...'

'Jonathan,' I cried, 'no. I will not listen. You are beside yourself with rage. You don't know what you say, or you never could say such cruel things. I will never marry you.'

He brought his right hand from behind his back, and I saw the pistol — I think my mother screamed again and started forward, but it was Denby who threw himself before me and received the full impact of the shot and fell at my feet.

I saw the blood seeping from his shoulder and breast, tried to stifle it with the skirt of my white dress, lifted his head on my arm, as once, many years ago, he had lifted mine. And Jonathan stood, white-faced, as he had as a boy, staring down at his brother.

He dropped the pistol to the floor, he covered his face with his hands.

'Denby,' he cried, 'Den — I didn't mean to shoot. I only meant to frighten Sally for what she has done ... I did not mean to hurt you or anyone. Denby — why doesn't he answer? For God's sake, is he dead?'

'No.' I pointed to a door on the other side of the room. 'That is a service door. You might get away unseen. Go back to the Hall and stay there. Say nothing. I will send for your mother but do not let her leave until my messenger arrives and you must be there to be seen by him. I will make them believe it was an accident — your mother has more than enough to bear without your being apprehended.'

He looked at me wildly, and then plunged out through the service door, closing it behind him. I prayed no one would see him leave.

There was the sounds of steps and voices outside, a knock on the door — I looked across at my mother and suddenly we were acting as we had never acted before to save Denby's life and Jonathan's freedom. She sprang out of her shocked, silent horror and threw the door open, crying that there had been an accident, that Sir Denby had been showing us the pistol, thinking it was not loaded.

People crowded into the open door — waiters and maids, and then the landlord, white and terrified. They stood staring open-mouthed. I was glad I was an actress. I was glad I had worked for my living since I was a child, and had known danger, fear and poverty, that I had been tempered to think and act, and not cry and flutter like a well-bred young lady. I took charge, making them do my bidding.

'Get these people out,' I said. 'All except two men to help me lift him — send for a doctor at once. Tell him Sir Denby has been hurt in an accident. Say *an accident*,' I said fiercely. 'Get water and bandages ... hurry ...'

As they moved like scared sheep to do my bidding Denby's eyes opened, and looked up into mine. 'Don't leave me, Sarah,' he said.

'No,' I answered. 'Of course I won't. I won't leave you.'

'Am I going to die?'

'No,' I said, and I spoke in the same fierce voice that I had ordered the hotel people to do my bidding. 'No. I won't let you. I won't let you.' For I knew that if he did die that night it would be my fault even if Jonathan was held for his murder — indirectly, maybe, but mine and mine alone.

CHAPTER SIX

I stayed with Denby all that night. Fortunately there was a doctor living close by, and even more fortunately Dr. Granger proved to be a man of skill and wisdom, and discretion. He sent all the gaping hotel servants away, and started on the ugly business of extracting the bullet, which was deep in the flesh beneath the left shoulder joint, dangerously near the main artery. Denby was conscious although he had been given morphia. I felt the basin for the instruments, hand swabs and dressings, and when it was finished put my arm round Denby and held him against my shoulder. I longed passionately that he should be safe. He smiled, his old boyish smile, and fainted for loss of blood. The doctor raised him on a mound of pillows and covered him gently.

'He will come round,' the doctor said. 'Then give him this draught and then he will sleep. The wound is deep but not mortal — it will depend whether any fever sets in as it can do so easily. I cannot say. Indeed he is the last person to sustain such a shock. There is a condition here — nothing to do with this accident which puzzles me.' He regarded me uneasily, as though he was about to say something more about Denby. 'Are you related to him?'

'No.'

'Engaged — perhaps?'

'No, indeed. My name is Sarah Thring. I am an actress in Mr. MacFarren's company at the theatre.'

'You are a friend of the family?'

'I — I know them well. Sir Denby was in Sheffield and he asked my mother and me to call and see him this evening after the performance.'

We were in the private sitting-room, having left my mother to watch by Denby. I pointed to the table, which looked like a still-life by a Dutch master — flowers, glassware, wine, tumbled fruits — and among them the chased, silver-handled duelling pistol.

'Sir Denby had brought the pistol with him because there have been highwaymen on the road from Derbyshire lately. He was joking, saying it was not loaded, but he hoped it would be frightening enough to keep robbers away — and he was showing us how it worked, and it *was* loaded.'

I was using all my imagination and my training to make this sound convincing.

'I see,' he said, still hesitating, but not, apparently, from any disbelief in my story. 'He will need watching and nursing day and night for some days. Unfortunately it is difficult to find good nurses in the town.' He began to pack his bag, after meticulously washing his instruments and hands. 'It is a disgrace that this difficult work should be left in the hands of a lot of dirty old biddies or well-meaning amateurs.'

'Be sure my mother and I will stay with him until his mother arrives. I will write to Lady Sefton immediately and send it by fast post-chaise to Rollers Croft Hall — it is not more than thirty miles.'

The preoccupied, worried expression lifted from his face.

'Yes, that will be the best thing,' he said with relief. 'I will come tomorrow morning — but do not hesitate to send for me if you are anxious during the night, and I will come at once. But I should particularly like to see the poor boy's mother when she arrives.' He paused again, thoughtfully. 'Of course one must allow for shock, but there are some symptoms I don't quite understand.'

'He has always been delicate, I believe.'

'Delicate? Ha, yes! Well, I will be on my way.'

He looked at me with puzzled admiration, my white dress

was stained with blood, and my face pale with shock and weariness. 'Well, you are a very brave and able young lady. I do not think he could be in better hands. Good night to you now. Do not forget, I will come at once should he need me.'

I thanked him and saw him to the door. It was now well past midnight, and the inquisitive little crowd of inn servants had reluctantly gone away to their beds. I shut the door and went into the bedroom where Denby lay in a deep, drugged sleep with my mother sitting beside him.

'Poor boy, poor child,' she said worriedly. 'What a wicked thing to happen at all! That Jonathan is mad.'

'History does repeat itself,' I said grimly, and she coloured and her eyes filled with tears.

'Ah, that's a cruel thing to be saying to me, Sally. But it is true. For sure the Seftons are violent and overbearing. They will never stop to listen, and they can be unforgiving. It's their pride, you see. At least it was with Sir Gore, and it is with this young man. No good ever came to me from the Seftons. They jump to conclusions and act before they think, and then it's too late. That Jonathan! I never saw such eyes — he would have killed you but for this poor boy. Then he was sorry. Let's hope it won't be too late for him.'

'Don't say such things,' I said fiercely. I had to make myself believe Denby would be all right. The whole tragic story was my fault and I was overwhelmed by guilt. But guilt was no use to Denby. 'Mother, go home, dear, and get some rest. Get the people here to call a carriage. Then as early as you can tomorrow come back, and bring me a fresh dress to wear. I will sleep tomorrow morning while you watch — until his mother arrives.'

'I'll do all that,' she said, and pulled her shawl about her, tied her bonnet, and said apprehensively, 'I had rather not be here when Charlotte Sefton comes. She will know me for sure, and there is no point in her learning who you are now.'

'Well, come early then. As soon as it is light.'

She went and I sat by Denby's bedside. The candlelight played on his thick, silken fair hair, and as my mother had said, he looked only a boy. I took the hand lying on the counterpane between my own, the tears running down my face, and prayed as I had never prayed before that he would get better, and that no more harm should come to him or his family through me. I even prayed for Jonathan.

'I will do anything,' I said out loud, 'anything in the world, if only he recovers.'

I put my head down on his hand, and as the night wore on I must have slept a little, for when I woke a clock somewhere in the town was chiming five o'clock, and Denby's hand, instead of lying between mine was gently stroking my hair. As I touched his brow it felt very hot, and I sat up quickly, to find his eyes open, his pupils looking very dark and bright, and his cheeks burning. He was looking at me intently, and when I met his eyes, he smiled.

'Denby — are you better?'

He nodded, heavy-eyed, and I knew he was not. He was conscious, but he was not better.

'Jon?' he whispered. 'Did he get away?'

'Yes. I told them it was an accident.' I told him quickly what I had said about the highwaymen and a glint of laughter rose in his fevered eyes, and he shook his head reproachfully.

'You must not make me laugh, it hurts,' he said in his ghost of a voice. 'You have a gift of laughter, Sarah. Wait until I am better, Sarah, then we will laugh together.'

He lay back on the pillows, but was restless, tossing his head. I dipped a cloth in water and bathed his dry burning face. Presently started to talk in a low muttering voice, and I knew he was half in delirium. 'I shall get better very quickly. Now we are going to be married, I must be better soon. A sick bridegroom would be stupid, especially for such a beautiful bride.'

He groaned a little, and I knew his wound must be hurting very much now. The doctor had told me if it became very painful to give him a little laudanum and water, and I would have risen to do so, and to get more cold water to wipe his face, but he clung to my hand. 'I haven't told you all my plans, yet. I thought, if you would like it, we would be married quickly and quietly — and as soon as I could travel, we would go away ... not back to the Hall. Not yet. It is too full of unhappiness and mourning ... we would go somewhere beautiful, and be alone together ... would you like that, my darling ...'

'You must not talk,' I told him. 'You must be quiet.' I released my hand, and went to the ewer and poured water in the basin, added lavender water, and bathed his dry burning face. It seemed that what the doctor was afraid of had already begun — the wound was becoming infected as so often happened, and the doctors were powerless to prevent it. I poured a glass of water, sweetened it, and added a few drops of laudanum, which he took obediently, turning his face to kiss my hands as I held the cup to his lips.

'Now try and sleep. Your mother will be here in the morning.'

'When she comes,' he said eagerly, 'I will tell her we are to be married. Kiss me, Sarah ...' I bent and gently kissed his lips. What else could I do?

He slept restlessly this time, often crying out in pain and at flickering dreams. At dawn my mother returned, bringing me a clean holland dress of a darkish blue, and a white gauze neckchief. I said if she would sit and watch I would try to get some rest. I washed, and braided my hair as well as I could, changed my torn and blood-stained white dress, and lay down on a sofa in the private sitting-room, and in a second was fast asleep.

When I woke it must have been between nine and ten, for I could hear the bustle of the inn yard outside, the stamp of horses and the cries of the grooms. The door opened, and Lady Sefton came in wrapped in a black cloak, a mourning bonnet on her head. She was pale, and from the dark circles below her eyes, I guessed she had slept as little as I. Indeed she must have driven through the dawn to be here so soon.

I sprang to my feet as she came in, closing the door behind her.

'I came at once,' she said. 'The postboy arrived with your message at one o'clock. Jon had already been home an hour by then. He had ridden furiously all the way. He came across country to the house and unsaddled and stabled the horse himself, so that no one knew what time he arrived. He told me everything —' her anxious eyes were coldly grateful. 'We have to thank you for your quick wit and discretion. Is it safe for him? Does no one suspect?'

I shook my head, but gestured a warning, opened the door into the corridor, but no one was there — I then looked behind the serving door through which Jonathan had escaped on the previous night. But we were quite alone.

'Tell me,' she insisted, 'does anyone but ourselves know?' She was racked with anxiety for the son she loved so passionately. She had not yet even spoken of Denby, and then, as though she realised how heartless she would seem to me, said quickly, 'And Denby — how is he?'

'He is not well,' I said. 'He has a fever. I suspect the wound is poisoned. The doctor will be here again soon.' I told her the explanation we had given to the doctor and the landlord. 'They seemed to accept it,' I said wearily. 'I hope so. There was no question of calling a constable last night. I think no one saw Jon, and Denby is not well enough to be questioned now. He is wandering a little with the fever. I am glad you have come. Now with your permission I will leave you to look after your son.'

The bedroom door opened and Herself came bustling out with the empty ewer.

'Will you ring for some water, Sally darling, for the poor lad is parched like a desert?' She saw Lady Sefton and went white. The two women, so different in looks and temperament, in breeding — in every way — stared at each other. Charlotte Sefton recognised her old enemy immediately, and her black eyes went from my mother to me and back again. Her white face became whiter, and she drew in a long breath.

'So!' she said. 'That is who you are — Molly O'Brien's daughter. Bad stock from bad stock. Why did I not recognise you from the first?'

'Why should you? I have changed from the poor, thin, badly dressed little girl who came to plead with you four years ago,' I said. 'That was the day when all this started. If you had been kind to me then — and I only wanted just a little help or kindness — none of this would have happened. I said I would make you pay for your cruelty and I have — but it was not to be like this. You were the one I wished to hurt, not poor Denby. The only one of you who was kind to me, and who, poor boy, truly loves me. I never meant that he should be hurt.'

'And what of Jonathan?'

I met her eyes — as hard as she was. 'I did not want this to happen. But Jonathan is as over-riding and cruel as you, and I did not care whether he was hurt or not — so long as I got my way.'

And then for the first time I seemed to have frightened her, for she drew back a little, her cold dark eyes troubled. A short while ago I would have triumphed at this, my pride and my temper would have been satisfied, but now if I could have undone what had happened — at almost any cost — I would have done so.

My mother was curiously subdued and humble. She put the jug down and went into a corner of the room and stood there shyly, twisting the corner of her apron like some servant girl who has been caught stealing. She could not meet Charlotte Sefton's eyes.

The tears welled up in my eyes and ran unchecked down my cheeks.

'You weep like a tragedy queen,' said Lady Sefton scornfully. 'Will you leave us in peace now? Are you satisfied with the consequences of your scheming?'

I was too tired and too guilty to flare back at her again.

'I have to ask your forgiveness, Lady Sefton,' I said. 'I have wronged you, and your sons. I swore I would do so when you spoke to me that day when I was a girl of sixteen. You hurt me bitterly and I wanted you to suffer. The way I planned was to ensnare your son and marry him, and perhaps send you away to live in some small dower-house while I queened it at the Hall. It has not turned out as I imagined. Jonathan was not the heir, and I could not dupe, deceive and tease poor Denby who is so gentle and kind, and now because of me, lies at death's door. I have lost my wish to belong to my father's family or to have a share in their fortune. I have lost my self-respect also, and the love of someone whom I have come to care about very greatly.'

For the first time my mother looked up, questioningly, puzzled, searching my face. But she did not speak.

I spread my hands helplessly. 'I never dreamed it would come to this,' I cried. 'I do not expect your forgiveness ... but God willing I hope for it one day.' I picked up my silken shawl and wrapped it round my head and shoulders. 'Come, Mother. We must get home to our lodgings to rest. I have a performance tonight and must not miss it. We can leave Denby safely in your hands, Lady Sefton.'

We went to the door, and as we reached it, I remembered something else.

'In his fever,' I said, 'he thinks that we are to marry — he talks about it whenever he wakes.'

'Yes, indeed,' said my mother speaking for the first time. 'He did just now, the poor child.'

'It is not true, Lady Sefton. I came here last night expressly to refuse his offer, and not, as Jon imagined, to consent. But he is too ill for me to tell him this now ... when he is better, perhaps you will explain.'

I had reached the door before she spoke.

'The Seftons are either lambs or tigers, as that woman there should have warned you. Jonathan cannot bear not to come first — it was his tragedy that he was not the eldest. Mine too, perhaps. Miss Thring — I cannot bring myself to call you Sefton any more than I could ever call your mother there my lady. Miss Thring, if Denby lives and becomes well I may be able to forgive you for all this, especially if our ways lie apart.'

'Of that at least I can assure you,' I said wearily. 'In a few days we shall leave this town, and I hope never to see you or any of your family again.'

We went back to our lodgings. There was no word from Robert. The landlady regarded us with curiosity as she served our midday meal for the story of the mysterious shooting had spread all over the town and caused great speculation. Controlling my anger, I gave her my version, in the hope that it would soon go over the garden wall to her next-door neighbour, and thence on down into the town.

She looked very relieved.

'I am glad to hear what you say, Miss Sally,' she said, 'because they've been talking about murder and suicide and all kinds of wild things. I told them, I said to the woman who brings eggs and chickens to the door, I said, my Miss Sally Thring is a real young lady, and would never be mixed up in anything like that.'

I was too tired to care very much. I lay down and slept like one stunned until my mother roused me in time to go to the theatre. MacFarren had been, she said, and taken some tea with her, but from her breath I guessed it had been spiced with something stronger. She still looked at me with that beaten, evasive look, with which she had stood silent before Lady Sefton. MacFarren had told her that wild rumours were going about the town, the most accepted that Denby had shot himself because I had refused him.

'I told him the truth of it.'

'The truth?' I asked grimly. 'What truth?'

'Ah, the truth we all decided upon this morning, for sure. And good man that he is he's gone back to the town to tell everyone and to try and get a bit into the news-sheet to that effect. Come now, darling, we must go or you'll be late on stage and that'll start more rumours.'

I looked at my tragic face in the mirror, and rubbed rouge into my cheeks. I put on a pretty dress of dove-coloured silk with a straw bonnet lined with pink silk, lace frills and coquettish little rosebuds. I wanted to give the impression that I did every night — a successful, pretty young actress, to whom nothing untoward or tragic had ever happened.

The hackney we hired every evening to take us to the theatre arrived but even in my cool silk I was too hot. My mother leaned back in the carriage, fanning herself with a little black fan — it was with such gestures, infinitely charming and coquettish, I realised how pretty she had been once. Fat, tired, anxious she might be, but she spread the little fan over her pretty hand elegantly. She did not talk at all, absorbed in her thoughts, occasionally glancing at me in silent anxiety. I wished she would talk — the garrulous brogue, which so often irritated me, would have been comforting, for I longed to be distracted from my agonising remorse. We drove down to the theatre together like two mutes.

The crowds of poor working people in the town depressed me; the women huddling into their shawls, the men sitting on their haunches outside the taverns. The new factories towered around everywhere. The clattering of clogs, the hot streets were full of dust and chaff and the shouting of the draymen. I thought of poor Denby and his dream that we should go away together to somewhere beautiful and peaceful. The heat was still intense, but with lowering sulphurous clouds reflecting the ruddy light of blast furnaces and trapping the belching smoke of the mill chimneys under a leaden ceiling of sullen cloud. Lightning still flashed but no storm broke, and the air was heavy and acrid and foul.

The house was packed. MacFarren was nervous, indeed the whole company were. I did not go to the green room, but when I went down to the stage some of the company glanced at me coldly. MacFarren told me to play calmly, that he did not think there would be any trouble.

The house was noisy and inattentive during the opening, and my first appearance was greeted with pandemonium, my admirers and supporters applauding, the people who had heard the rumours that a young Derbyshire squire had attempted suicide for love of me hissing and booing, and in a few moments fighting broke out in the pit.

I played on desperately, hoping that calm would come, that people would become interested in the play, but it was no use. MacFarren rang down the curtain, appealed for order without any result. I went to my dressing-room and sat down, too tired and tense to care. Everything had come to a climax. Even the one thing that I could trust, my work, seemed to have come to an end. And my mother was not there. I knew what she was when danger or any unpleasantness threatened, running away like a guilty frightened child. I sat in the dressing-room in my paint and garish stage costume, wondering if the old weakness had tempted her and what inn she was hiding in, and with what company. There had been times when I was a child when I had gone from inn to inn, wrapped in my shawl, looking for her, frightened and hungry. But lately she had been so good and reliable — only today, since seeing Lady Sefton, had that old look of fear and doubt come back to her.

The sound of the shouting round the theatre and in the auditorium was drowned by a terrific crash of thunder, and immediately afterwards the welcome noise of heavy rain, pouring down over the town. The air cooled miraculously.

Presently MacFarren came in and told me he had called the constables, that the hooligan element had been cleared and the drenching rain was dousing the tempers of the crowds outside. I went back and he led me on to the stage to a polite ripple of applause. I worked as I had never worked before that night, playing the witty, foolish Lady Teazle with every bit of charm and technique that I could muster, although inwardly I was tired, sad, unhappy. In this at least I would show them what I could do.

The applause at the end rewarded me. I felt as I stood there bowing that I had achieved something. When I left the stage the company gave me a round of applause, the resentment had gone from their eyes. I had passed a test — and however much life might frighten me, an audience never would again.

When I returned to the dressing-room I found my mother waiting for me, her bonnet and shawl soaking wet from the storm. But she was quite sober, and I was ashamed of my fears for her. She told me that she had guessed that I was waiting for a message from London and that she had been to the coachyard to see if a letter waited at the office there, or anything had come by the evening stage-coach. But there had been no letter for me.

'It's that Mr. Robert Thornton, isn't it, Sally? You've been hoping to hear from him again.'

I told her that I had written to him twice. I did not tell her of that foolish boastful announcement that I had achieved my purpose and soon would be Lady Sefton, and which I wished I had never written. I could spend my time now wishing I had not done so many stubborn and reckless things.

'Should I not go to London for you, Sally?' she asked eagerly. 'I am not playing at all this week, a coach starts early tomorrow — I could go and enquire after Mr. Thornton, and ask him if he has received your letter.'

'Letters,' I said shamefacedly. 'And if you see him, Mama, tell him he was right, and I am truly sorry, and will he forgive me. That is all. I — I don't expect him to come and see me, or —' and by now the tears were running down my face — 'or ever want to see me again, for that matter. But I would like him to know I am sorry.'

'Ah, then, Alannah,' she said, putting her plump arms about me. 'He'll be forgiving you, I am sure. He always was a fine, quiet, kind gentleman.'

'Oh, Mama, be quiet. I know that. It's just that they can't be undone now. All these dreadful things I've done.'

'Well, you've not to worry now. I'll be there and back here within a few days — and, who knows, perhaps Mr. Thornton will return with me?'

I looked at her with renewed hope. I knew it was not the sort of thing a young lady should do, but I was beyond convention since Denby had been shot. I felt increasingly that I was being caught in a trap of my own making, and I had to know if Robert had received my second letter.

'It's a long, tiring journey for you — to go there and straight back here.'

'Ah, get off with you. It's nothing for an old trouper like myself. Sure when we were with Roland we walked nearly that distance behind the carts at times.'

We went back to our lodgings so that she could change and pack a small bag, and get a few hours' rest, and early the following morning I saw her on to the coach for London.

I went to rehearsal, but I still felt nervous and anxious, weighed down with inner distress. All my mad, bad schemes and plans had been abandoned, and I had not heard from Robert. I knew that however hard I worked — indeed, however great my success — I was not the consummate and dedicated actress to whom this life was sufficient. These past weeks had brought me down to the real inner core of me, a lonely girl of twenty, exhausted with battling against life, disgusted with her own selfish ambitions, longing for the reassurance of love.

Mr. MacFarren saw I was tired and nervous, so did not keep me long, telling me to stop worrying and get some rest. He had seen the editor of the local paper, who had published a paragraph deploring the behaviour of certain members of the public who had rioted in the theatre last night, incensed by completely unfounded rumours. We would have no trouble tonight, he was quite sure.

He was right — the performance went smoothly enough, and the house again was full. The audience was sympathetic to me, and because of my performance the night before, my group of admirers had grown.

When I got back to the dressing-room there were the usual bouquets, and notes from admirers. I opened them absently, until the last one — it was from Lady Sefton, asking me to call and see her at The Falcon.

I knew then that this was what I was most dreading. I had known in my heart that my responsibility for what had happened had not ended, and I was terrified that perhaps Denby had grown worse, and that he might be dying. I hurriedly changed into my street clothes, bade the dresser order me a carriage, and drove round to the inn.

Lady Sefton was waiting for me in the sitting-room, and when I asked how Denby was she said he was still very ill. The doctor said the next few days would tell if he would recover.

'Sit down, Sarah.' It was the first time she had called me by my name, and I took a chair, awed and silent, like a reprimanded child. She was still wearing black, but had a white lace cap on her dark hair. I could see now that it was heavily streaked with grey. Something had gone from her since I had seen her before. The fierceness and the pride. There was a frightening resignation about her, which at first I could not understand.

I could hear movements in the bedroom beyond, and she told me that Mrs. Ridstone was now with her to help with the nursing, because it might be weeks before Denby could be moved.

'He calls for you whenever he is awake, Sarah. He says it is all arranged, that you are engaged to be married, and that you are to be married at once . . . and he is in such a state of anxiety because he has not seen you for two evenings. He thinks this is my doing. That I have sent you away and forbidden you to see him. Will you go to him now and reassure him that this is not so.'

'Have you told him the truth about me? That I am Sir Gore's daughter, and his cousin, and the reason why I wished to marry Jonathan?'

She looked at me with a flash of old scorn. 'I have told him everything, including the fact which I told you before — who can be sure you are Sir Gore's child?'

'My mother swore this is true.'

She shrugged, did not comment: her opinion of my mother was obvious. But she did not let me speak. 'Whatever I say, Sarah, makes no difference to Denby. I am defeated.' She met my eyes and this time there was nothing but a real and terrible appeal for my help. 'I truly believe he will die without you. You will see him now?'

I said desperately, 'Lady Sefton — if I do, he will believe I am going to marry him. I am fond of him, sorry, bitterly sorry for all I have done. But I love someone else, and even if I cannot marry this person, I do not feel it would be fair to Denby — when he is better . . .'

'He will never be better without you, Sarah. He will not even try. He is not naturally strong. As a child he was always a source of anxiety to me. We were poor then, when Sir Gore was alive and you lived at Rollers Croft. I could not afford to care properly for such a delicate child when we moved from lodging to lodging as the regiment moved.'

I could not believe what she told me, or rather I did not want to believe it. That a young man like Denby could not recover, or rather did not want to recover. Then I remembered how he had said, 'There has never been anyone but you, Sarah,' and I knew she was speaking the truth.

'Sarah, I am sharing your remorse now. I have always loved Jonathan the best. I have always wished him to inherit Rollers Croft, and indeed trained him to do so — to be the master one day. Denby has always been weak and delicate, subject to unaccountable illness and infections. I was so proud of my strong handsome son — so ashamed of my weak one. Well, I have been punished. We have both been punished, Sarah. But I must make Denby's life as happy as I can, and it seems he cannot be happy without you — I am asking you to marry him.'

'Lady Sefton, I do not love Denby. The trouble I have already caused between him and his brother is enough. I cannot marry him.'

She sighed and rose, smoothing down her rich, silken black gown in a queer, resigned, helpless way, touching in one so strong and hard.

'I was afraid you would say that,' she said. 'Well, I can only ask you, if you will not be my son's wife, if you will be the consummate actress that you are — and come every day to see him, and reassure him that you will marry him, that I have not sent you away, that all will be well. Then, perhaps, if the fever goes and he recovers I can tell him the truth and that you were only deceiving him for his own good.'

'I cannot,' I said again.

'You will not refuse to see him now? You could not be so cruel?'

She was right. I went into the bedroom, and when I saw him, lying watching the door, waiting for me, and the way his face lit up with joy, what could I do? I could no more have killed that joy and relief than I could have been cruel to any weak and helpless creature. He was very ill, and the fever was high. I sat by him, silent most of the time, smiling as he talked, and made plans for our future.

He had talked with the doctor, he said, who had thought that Italy was the best place for him to recover in. There was no reason why he should not live permanently abroad if he wished. Jonathan and his mother would run Rollers Croft. He would tell his mother to instruct their lawyers to find a pleasant villa somewhere facing the sun and overlooking the sea for us. He would be better in a few weeks. We must make arrangements to marry immediately — and then we could go to our new home. He would try very hard to recover quickly, and be a model patient, because it would be better if we could be in Italy before the winter came.

'I have asked Mother to bring some of the family jewellery,' he told me eagerly. 'There is nothing here in the town that I would wish to buy you. The day before the accident I searched the shops, and could find nothing. Now we can go ahead with all the arrangements.'

I told him not to hurry. That there was plenty of time, that he must think of getting well, and then we could make plans.

'I shall never get well unless you promise, Sarah,' he said. 'You are such an unpredictable girl. If I let you go for a moment you might vanish into thin air. I can't forget that you did that once before. And why should we wait?'

His thin, flushed face smiled up at me with a look of such pure confidence that I could have burst into tears. 'I know if we marry I shall get well. But if I don't, what does it matter? You will have made me happy — and I shall be able to give you all the things I long to give you and which you deserve.'

And then, I really did cry, and it was he who dried my tears.

The following day, after the performance, I called at the hotel again, and he was much better. He still had some fever and was weak, but the pain had greatly decreased, but all his anxious restlessness had gone. He was waiting calmly for me to come, quite confident that everything was settled, and we were to be married. The only promise he made me give was that I should come every evening to see him without fail. He had sent for his attorneys to make arrangements about settlements and the legal side of the marriage. I looked desperately at his mother, but she merely shook her head, gesturing me to silence, whispering that in a day or so, when he was really better, I could leave.

True to his promise a servant brought jewels from Rollers Croft Hall. There was a fine diamond that he insisted on my accepting and wearing. When I left each evening I gave it to his mother, only putting it on when I went into the room. I prayed for my mother to come back and that Robert would come with her, giving me strength to break the truth to Denby. I prayed for Denby's recovery so that there was no need for me to continue in this tragic masquerade.

And every day when the London coach came in I went to see if my mother had returned by it.

She came in on the Friday evening, and I knew as soon as I saw her face that the journey had been useless. She told me that Robert had gone away suddenly some weeks ago, and neither his office nor Mrs. Billings knew exactly where, except that it was abroad. And that he had left no word for me. I had sent my letters to his private lodgings, not to his Chambers in Grays Inn, so with a great deal of blarney and a little bribery Mother had persuaded Mrs. Billings to look through the correspondence awaiting him there, and there was one letter from me. I saw at once he had received my first letter, and in disgust and despair of my ever coming to my senses had gone away. That in all probability I would not see or hear from him again. I could make no further appeal.

We walked to the theatre together, my face set and cold, my mother murmuring words of comfort, telling me not to worry, to write again, that he would have to return some time, and would think differently when he saw me. That I was but a young girl with plenty of years and conquests before me, and that there were as good fish in the sea as on land.

I cut her short. 'I cannot leave Sheffield until Denby recovers,' I said.

I went to see him after the performance as I had done the past three nights. My mother waited outside in the carriage. Lady Sefton rose to greet me as I came in.

'He is much better,' she said. 'The fever has subsided. The wound is clean and beginning to heal. In a few days he will be able to travel. He is pressing me to make positive arrangements for you to be married. So, Sarah, now you will have to decide — it is entirely in your hands. Whether you tell him, as you have told me, that you cannot go on with it. Or whether you will try to make amends for all the pain and harm you have brought on me and mine.'

I said I would tell him the truth, and went into the room to do that, but when I saw him looking so frail and white, though clear-eyed and free of fever, my heart failed again. And then, I thought, what did it matter now?

We were married the following week at the parish church near Rollers Croft Hall. My mother was not there — I sent her back to London with the company, saying I would see her there shortly, and hear her plans for her future. Whether she would stay in England or travel abroad with Denby and myself. Mr. MacFarren would keep her with the company. He had, I realised, become attached to her and his friendship was a comfort. He assured me that if ever I made a decision to return to the boards he would be delighted to welcome me back.

I would not have returned to Rollers Croft for the wedding if I had thought I would see Jonathan there, but when he heard of our intentions he left immediately for the house in London. I was longing to get away from England, because I dreaded the thought of seeing him again.

Felicia was at the Hall, however, and although she was not happy, there was a small new hope about her. At least if Jonathan did not love her, he was not going to marry me. She told me he was in a terrible state when he had returned.

'He kept saying that if Denby died it would be murder.' She hesitated, then said with difficulty, 'Sarah, keep out of his way. He is full of remorse over Denby, because although they disagreed they were in some ways very close. But he blames you for everything. He thinks you care for no one but yourself and becoming Lady Sefton.'

'With reason,' I said grimly.

'Yes, but his own tempers and passion are to blame too. His conceit and pride. It's strange, but I who know him so very well, and know how bad he is, love him more than anyone.'

'Poor Cia.'

'No. For the first time I have been able to help him. While he was here he devoted himself to handling the affairs of the house and estate while his mother was in Sheffield with Denby. I used to help Sir Hayden when he was alive. I write a good hand and have a head for figures — I should have made a good clerk . . . so

I was quite close to him, although, as a girl, I might just as well not exist for Jon.'

'You are very good, Cia.'

She sighed, folded her hands, and smiled wanly. 'Jonathan will come back here as soon as you leave for London, for there is much to see to here, and though he is wild, and spends his nights in bad company, he is a good manager. I suppose that is his trouble — Rollers Croft is what he cares about most and it is not his.'

She loved Jonathan with such a touching acceptance — so uncritically. I wondered if in time he would become aware of her devotion and forget about me — if he ever loved me. Perhaps I was just like the house and title — something he wanted and could not have.

'I am glad you are not to marry Jonathan,' she said, 'but I cannot understand you marrying Denby . . . apart from the title and the money . . .'

'It is not that — believe me it is not that.' I rose restlessly, and repeated, 'It is not that, believe me, Cia, however it might look and whatever Jonathan may think . . .' I said, 'It was just that it meant so much to Denby. His mother thought it meant his life. And nothing matters so much to me any more.'

The wedding was in the little parish church which stood within the grounds of the Hall. There was Lady Sefton, Cia, myself and Mrs. Ridstone. Mrs. Ridstone, who had always been very fond of me, was to travel with us on our long journey. Denby was helped into a carriage and driven to the church. He seemed to gain a little strength every day and I began to hope that, if I cared for him, in the warmer air and sunshine of Italy he would recover completely.

It was not really like a wedding. I wore my dove-coloured dress and pink lined bonnet, and carried a handful of pink roses from the gardens — I bought no special clothes, and neither would I take any of the Sefton jewels.

'You will be enough of a responsibility,' I told Denby that night after dinner as he sat propped up with cushions, holding my hand. 'My chief occupation will be looking after you and I don't want the bother of a lot of jewellery. Let us just think of getting away to our new home, and making you quite well again.'

'In Italy I will buy you beautiful things,' he said. 'Cameos, corals, and pearls, and we will go and see the great pictures and buildings, and Rome and Florence ... everything.' I wished that the concern and tenderness I felt for him had really been love.

I spent my wedding night alone in the same room I had occupied when I had first come to Rollers Croft, and Denby slept in a small communicating room. He no longer needed watching during the night, but he had to sleep propped up on pillows to make sure the wound continued to drain successfully. I woke once or twice, and put on my gown and crept in to see how he was, and that first strange wedding night he slept deeply and restfully in great peace.

The following day we left for London in the Seftons' largest carriage. I was grateful that Mrs. Ridstone came with me, for she was a competent nurse, and very sensible. We had to go by very easy stages — stopping for a rest at midday, and staying each night at a different hotel. We stopped at Market Harborough, Bedford and St. Albans and arrived on the third day in London, and went directly to the house in Farm Street near Berkeley Square.

It was the first time I had been in the house in Farm Street. Denby descended slowly from the carriage with the help of the footman. His left arm, where the wound was beneath his shoulder, was still strapped across his chest, his right arm rested across my shoulders.

As always the exertion made him a little breathless — the wound had barely missed his lung — so we made slow progress up the steps and into the long hall of the London house. A butler opened a door into a large reception room on the ground floor, a well-appointed room with many portraits and fine furniture and at the far end standing before the high marble chimneypiece, Jonathan was waiting for us.

I caught my breath — I had been told he would leave London on the same day that we left Rollers Croft. He must have waited deliberately to see us.

He looked different, haggard and thin. The whites of his blue eyes were slightly bloodshot, as though he had been drinking heavily. But he was still as handsome, still as splendidly dressed, with his powerful assured stance. He looked directly at his brother, but not at me, and did not speak until Denby had been settled in a chair and the butler had left the room.

I stood silently, untying my bonnet strings, wishing myself anywhere but with these two young men whose lives I had so nearly ruined. It was Denby who spoke first, stretching out his hand.

'Well, Jon, don't we shake hands?'

The colour flared in Jon's face, and he took Denby's hand.

'I stayed to see you. It may be a long time before we meet again. I am leaving for home at once. I shall go by coach to Derby tonight. I — I wanted to ask your forgiveness, Denby.'

'Jonathan — it is not my forgiveness you have to ask.'

Jonathan did not reply.

'Let us all forget it if we can,' said Denby. 'I know you love Sarah, and how you must have felt. We are all driven to do things which we don't intend to do, and regret immediately. Sarah knows that as well as you, Jonathan. You have heard from Mother that Sarah is really our cousin — that she felt we owed her a debt, as indeed we do.'

'I have heard,' said Jonathan.

'When we were boys,' said Denby, 'you always won — until now. Now I have won at last and Sarah is my wife. Cannot we forget the past and part friends?'

'You stopped me from committing murder, I have to thank you for that,' said Jonathan. But he still did not look at me, or ask my forgiveness.

'How long to you intend to remain abroad?' he asked.

'As long as we please, until I am better. Perhaps for ever,' said Denby. 'It depends if Sarah is happy there.'

'I will leave you to talk,' I said. 'There is a great deal to attend to. The courier is coming tonight with the details of our journey... so if you will excuse me.'

Denby smiled, touched my hand as I passed. Jonathan

bowed stiffly. As I turned to close the door I met his eyes for the first time and drew back, startled.

I went up to my room and found Mrs. Ridstone laying out my night things and a dress for me to change into for dinner. It was early evening, so I changed, did my hair and went down, thinking to help Denby up the stairs, for he would have a light meal served in his room. Stairs were one of his most difficult problems.

When I went into the drawing-room, Jonathan was there alone. He stood looking at me, then said abruptly, 'Your husband has been helped upstairs.'

'I will go to him,' I said.

'Wait, let me look at you.' He turned me round to face him, his eyes searching my face. 'You are still as beautiful, Sarah. And now you have everything you gambled for. You are Lady Sefton, and Denby has control of everything. You can scheme to send my mother and me away from Rollers Croft as your father sent my parents away.'

'And as they sent my mother and myself away,' I answered. 'No, Jonathan, the thought of living at the Hall is unbearable to me now. I never want to live there — my only comfort in this is that we shall be far away. You have nothing to fear from me.'

He stood back, and said, 'I do not believe you. You have fooled me, jilted me and nearly driven me to murder. Nothing you can say or do will make me believe that you are not selfish, cruel and false. But, God help me, I still want you, and I envy poor Denby as I have never envied him before.'

He picked up his hat and gloves and went towards the door. As he passed me he raised his hand as though he would strike me across the face, but he just flicked the gloves across my lips before he went out.

I went up to my husband. He was sitting at a table by the window, and the footman was laying a meal, and I said I would eat there with him. When the man was out of the room, Denby said with a smile, 'You look so lovely tonight, Sarah. When we get to Italy we shall be together in every way. We shall share our nights as well as our days, because I shall be strong again and our honeymoon will begin. We shall really be lovers, Sarah.'

And I wished we could always remain as we were — tender and affectionate friends.

Next morning I drove to Grays Inn Road to say goodbye to my mother. I drove there in our private carriage with two manservants on the box, and a pair of high-stepping bays, and as I drove along Holborn, all the old sights and the smell of London came back to me, and I wished that I was living in Grays Inn Road with Herself, just young Sally Thring, the aspiring young actress, with all her life before her, and none of the awful implications of passion and revenge shadowing my life.

At our lodgings Mrs. Billings let me in, curtsying — big-eyed at the fine carriage waiting at the kerb. I went up to our rooms, which I had arranged for my mother to keep for her home while I was away.

I opened the door into our sunny parlour, and Herself was standing by the fireplace, white-faced and shaken-looking, and beside her was Robert Thornton. Suddenly I was trembling and my heart racing in my breast. He turned and looked at me in anger and distress.

'Sarah,' he cried, 'I have just returned from France this morning and received your letters, I came here immediately and your mother has told me you have married Denby Sefton. My God, Sally, tell me it isn't true.'

I held my arms out to him and cried out like a child. 'Where have you been? Why did you go away when I needed you? Why didn't you come to me?'

I stumbled and would have fallen if he had not caught me and helped me to a chair. My mother still stood silently staring at us. I had put an insuperable barrier between us and nothing, not even his dear presence, could help me now.

CHAPTER SEVEN

I wondered if, after today, Robert and I would ever meet again. I could not understand why I had not realised before just how much I loved him. I suppose I must have been blind to everything but my ambitions, which had been so nearly in my grasp.

But now I became aware that there was something else, not yet said. There was some other cause for my mother's distress.

'Sarah — I went to France on your behalf,' he said gravely. 'To make some enquiries about your father...'

'My father? My father is dead.'

'Yes, Sarah. Your father is dead — but not of a bullet wound in a duel at Rollers Croft. By a fever in Martinique two years ago.'

I looked at him uncomprehendingly and then at my mother, who said timidly, 'Sally, you must forgive me. Whatever I did was for you. Lies breed lies and trouble. But whatever I did I was only a girl at the time, and in great need and distress.'

'You are telling me I am not Sir Gore Sefton's daughter?'

'You are the daughter of Gerard Danjoy,' Robert said quietly.

'A bastard — as Lady Sefton hinted?' I faltered.

'No,' my mother protested, 'we were married. We went to Dublin together to be married by a priest. Without permission from Gerard's family — I had none to ask. No one knew. We only had my earnings at the theatre. Then when the French wars ended he went back to tell his family, and never came back. Not until you were ten, and then you know what happened.'

The tears were running down her face. She told how she was pregnant and penniless, and Sir Gore was pressing her to marry him, tenacious, overpowering, pursuing her as ruthlessly as Jonathan had pursued me. She gave in; she married him and let him think that the child born seven months later was his.

'I was very ill, it was said I was brought to bed early; I let them believe it. It meant that you would be a lady, not dragged up in lodgings off Drury Lane.'

I rose, my mind in a whirl. 'But you swore, Mama... you swore to me that I was Sir Gore's daughter. That day when I went to Rollers Croft and Lady Sefton turned me away. You swore on your rosary.'

'Ah, I did, I know I did, indeed, and it was wicked of me, and many a penance I've done for it. But when you came back that day, all white and distressed, child that you were, what could I do? Your pride had been hurt enough. What harm could it do for you to think yourself well-born? Which indeed you are, for Gerard was a fine gentleman.'

'Oh, Mama, Mama... why did you do it?'

'And how was I to know you'd get mad ideas into your head and carry them through? For all I knew we were finished with the Seftons. And what I had done was against the law, as Mr. Thornton will tell you. It was bigamy. My darling, I'm never one for thinking, and I've never had much luck, and I thought it would be all right in the end.'

The gentle, cajoling, blarneying voice edged my nerves. I did not blame her — I never had, uneducated child of the streets that she was. I knew she never thought of the future, just told the first lie that came to hand. I excused her, but I could never excuse myself.

'Hush,' I said. 'Hush, Mama. Don't cry — I was more to blame.'

I rose, wandering blindly about the room. I felt dazed. All these things I had done, hurting people, setting them against each other. I had thought I had every right to share in the Seftons' fortune. But I had no right at all. I was an impostor from the start. I had no reason, no excuse for anything I had done.

'You asked me what I have done,' I said hopelessly. 'I have done irreparable harm to many people, and myself, and nothing can undo it now.'

There was none of the tender indulgence with which Robert used to look at me, and when he spoke his voice had no warmth, no affection for me.

'Sarah, I went to France to try and help you. I suspected from the dates of parish records that Sir Gore was not your father. If I could prove it to you, your mad ambition to become Lady Sefton would be pointless. But I did not dream you would marry Denby.'

'I did not want to, nor mean to. I said I would not. But he was so ill, his mother and the doctor both said he would not try to recover ... It meant so much to him and ...' I stopped, unable to tell him now that if he had received my letter and come to me I would have told him I loved him. I just said helplessly, 'It meant so little to me and so terribly much to him ... and it was all my fault ...'

'Not at all,' he said shortly. 'These things never are. It all began with Lady Charlotte being cruelly heartless to you and your mother years ago. And, ironically, you did not need the money. Danjou came into his family fortune, and settled money on your mother. Not a great income, but enough. After Sir Gore's death he dare not return to England and your mother changed her name. Danjou died without tracing her, but I will see that she receives this money now.'

'All this would have made so much difference once —' A cry was torn from me: 'Everything comes too late.'

I wanted to get away. I could not endure Robert's presence. If he had ceased to love me, I deserved it — if he still did, then it was an agony for both of us which I could not bear. I kissed my mother and said goodbye to her — it might be many months before I saw her again. She had been feckless and foolish but who was I to blame her? I had committed worse follies with less reason, through selfish pride and ambition, while she had only been weak, timid and kind.

'When do you sail?' he asked.

'On Friday. We travel to Southampton on Thursday and will go aboard that night.'

'May I call tomorrow? There are matters to arrange for your mother's welfare while you are away. I will need your address in Italy. It is essential that I can get in touch with you.'

'You are coming as my lawyer — not as my friend?'

'As both, I hope,' he said quietly, and for the first time a touch of the old tenderness showed in his voice and eyes.

I gave him my hand with all the dignity I could muster and then drove back to Farm Street. Denby was waiting anxiously for my return.

'I always worry,' he said, 'if you are late — I shall not be happy until we get away.'

I had called in a doctor to see Denby during the few days we were in London. He was a fashionable person, with an impressive bedside manner, who made me long for the unpretentious Dr. Granger of Sheffield. There was no fever he assured me, but the pulse was a little fast — in the warm air of Italy all would be well.

Robert called as he had promised, and now I had my emotions well under control. We arranged my mother's affairs — she would keep our rooms at Grays Inn Road, and work with MacFarren if she wished. Robert promised to call regularly, and to write to me about her occasionally, for she could scarcely sign her name and I had always written her letters.

When everything was settled, Robert asked if I had told Denby about my parentage, and I shook my head.

'My mother is secure, that is a great relief. Thank you for that. I do not have to ask for money for her. But for me, it makes no difference.' I drew in a deep breath and raised my eyes. 'Denby sincerely loves me. I have married him. All I can do now is to devote myself to his health and happiness.'

For a moment Robert did not speak, but when he did there was a little break in his voice. 'Whatever you are and have done, Sarah, no one can say you lack courage.'

I took him to Denby who had asked to see him. He greeted him warmly as my lawyer and friend, and said, unexpectedly, 'I would ask you a favour, Thornton, as a friend of Sarah's — and I hope of mine.'

'If you will tell me how I can help you?'

'Tomorrow we travel to Southampton, and sail the following day on the early tide. The one thing that has been on my mind is that Sarah has the responsibility of our journey. Mrs. Ridstone is good, but only a simple woman. Would you spare the day tomorrow, and travel down with us, and see to things which normally I would have undertaken? I don't wish to be an anxiety to Sarah on the way.'

Robert looked at me, and something in his face shook my heart. But he only said gravely, 'Of course I will come.'

Next morning we left London in the Seftons' carriage, Mrs. Ridstone following in a second vehicle with our luggage. We had not taken a great deal, thinking to buy what we wanted when we reached Genoa.

It was a long drive, and very tiring for Denby, and I was grateful for Robert's kind and watchful presence, his help at the stages when we changed horses or stopped for a meal. Indeed when we drove down to the quayside where the merchant ship lay, he put a strong arm round Denby, and half-lifted him from the coach and on to the deck.

We had a fine, large, airy state-room for a sitting-room during the day where we could take our meals if we wished. Robert settled Denby in a comfortable chair, and saw all our goods aboard. He refused Denby's invitation to take a meal with us, saying he must get back to London. He shook hands with Denby, who thanked him for his trouble.

'When we return to England,' said Denby, 'I shall carry Sarah ashore. You will see how well and strong I shall be. But thank you again, Thornton. I don't know how we should have managed without you.'

Robert turned to me, and I could not bear the moment of parting.

'I will come up on deck with you,' I said.

We went up on deck and walked slowly aft. The big three-master rocked gently on the tide, and the docks and the old town looked like a painting in the evening light. The captain and the supercargo were watching men carrying stores aboard and lowering them into the hold. On the quayside stood our carriage waiting to take Robert back to London.

We seemed to be alone — standing behind the deck-house. The tears were pouring down my face.

'I cannot bear to say goodbye,' I said. 'Not to you.'

'Sarah,' he said, and then as though in pain: 'My love, my

darling, my bad and crazy child...' He took me in his arms and kissed me — the second time he had kissed me, and this time, because I was thinking only of him and no longer had a head full of ambitious dreams, it was terrible and wonderful. Like being born into a new realisation of life. We kissed passionately, with a terrible, silent abandon. This was like no love-making I had known: this was adult, final and complete; if we had been quite alone then, we could not have separated. Until that moment I had been a vain, frivolous, thoughtless child and now at his touch I flamed into womanhood, my heart and soul awakened and crying for his love.

He put me away from him.

'I must go,' he said.

'I am sorry,' I said. 'Oh, Robert, I am so bitterly sorry for everything I have done. I have brought too much harm and sorrow to everyone, and now I must try to make amends.'

He touched my face and I turned my cheek against the warm, well-shaped hand, remembering how I had noticed his hands the first time we had met. 'I love you. Now you know. I always shall.'

'Poor Sarah,' he said, 'poor little reckless one. I cannot be the guardian of your conscience any more... you are alone now.'

We did not say goodbye. He stood for a long minute looking at me, my hair, my eyes, my lips, my slender sighing body, as though he was taking me into himself for ever. Then he turned and walked away from me along the deck.

I went to the side and watched him run lightly down the companionway to the quay, a tall, fine man, very distinguished in his dark lawyer's clothes, his hat in his hand, the sunlight touching the white wing in his black hair. He turned at the carriage door and looked up once more. It was not the grave face of a sober man of law, but the face of a young and passionate man, agonisingly in love. We stood for a long moment, looking across the glimmering harbour water, and then he got into the carriage and it clattered away over the cobbles, and I wondered if I would ever see him again. I stood, leaning my head against the deck-house, the sobs tearing my breast, and it was some while before I could control them.

I walked about in the evening air until my tears were dry and my breath and manner composed, and then I went below deck. Denby was unpacking some of his books and arranging them, and he looked up at me with his usual perceptive tenderness.

'Has Thornton gone?'

'Yes.'

'You were a long time.'

'I walked on deck for a while — you should come up before the sun sets. It is a lovely evening.'

'Yes, when I have done this.' He looked fixedly at a title, then pushed the volume into a shelf, and said, 'Thornton is a fine-looking man.'

'Yes, I think so,' I said non-committal.

'How did you meet him?'

For a moment I could not collect my thoughts — Robert seemed to have been in my life for ever. Then I said, 'He was in the coach that brought my mother and me to London when I came to take up my engagement at the Royalty Theatre. He has always been very kind and considerate to us.'

'Why not?' he said, meeting my eyes. 'He is in love with you.'

I made a gesture of protest, but he only smiled.

'I am not jealous, Sarah. He has gone now and we are together. I know that I must guard you closely, for many men will fall in love with you. You are that kind of woman — you emanate a fascination which you do not realise. But you are my wife.' He held out his hand. 'Come.' He led me to the door of the inner cabin. It was a spacious four-berth cabin, and on the small dressing-chest there was a beautiful bouquet of flowers. The two lower bunks were made up. My heart quickened a little — it would be the first time we had shared a room.

'We shall be together at last, Sarah,' he said. 'Now and through the voyage, and for ever. This is our real wedding night.'

I had said to Robert I must devote myself to his happiness, and now those words were no longer a promise but a reality which the night would bring.

All through the long, calm and beautiful voyage to Italy Denby continued to mend. By the time the brig had passed Gibraltar into the Mediterranean his health had improved so much and he looked better than I ever remembered. I was grateful for Mrs. Ridstone's presence and company, her solid Derbyshire good sense and faithful service. She was a tower of strength during those days.

I did not love Denby, but I had a deep affection for him, and he was so kind and gentle with me, a boy entranced with his first experience of love. And I, for all my surface sophistication, and theatrical self-confidence, was as young and unlearned as he.

At first I was nervous of him going ashore at the foreign ports, having been told that in the summer when water was short there were often virulent fevers in these towns. But by the time we had passed Valencia and were beating our way up towards Toulon in a fine sailing breeze he was so well that afterwards we always went ashore at every port of call — two very innocent and inexperienced tourists, exploring the strange and beautiful and sometimes sordid towns, guide books in hand, eyes wide at the strange people, scents, smells and food.

But I did feel happy for him, and I suppose any woman who is so openly and proudly loved and admired responds. It was not that I did not think of Robert Thornton — I thought of him always, but no longer with longing and passion. In a way I was like a nun — absurd analogy, because I was a young married woman — but I had entered this marriage like someone who has put the realities of life and sex away for ever.

We sailed into Genoa early in September, the great port basin full of rocking spars, its cliff-like buildings towering behind the town. The piled-up houses with their strings of brightly-coloured washing looked like bunting hung for some eternal carnival. The steep streets made me think of those colonies of sea-birds, nest upon nest, piled high on cliff shelves against the sky.

'My goodness,' I exclaimed, 'shall we live right up there?' The captain laughed, and told me that these were the narrow streets where the dock-workers and seafaring folk lived, but away from the harbour there was a spacious and rich town, with many beautiful villas, squares, churches and marble palaces. And this I found to be true.

An agent met us with a carriage and drove us out to our new home and we were entranced with its beauty. It was a small white villa, built in the Moorish style, with arcaded terraces and balconies, and gardens with paved walks and little artificial runnels of water and cool miniature fountains. Statues stood among the cypress trees. It was one of several such villas high above the coastal road. Behind the mountains climbed to the sky, protecting us from the cold north winds. Below us the sea stretched silver and blue to Africa, and the sun shone full upon our terraces and balconies from dawn to dusk. The vines were heavy with grapes when we arrived, and the gardens bright with zinnias and the gaudy flowers of autumn. The villa was called Casa di Lillas and all along the steep driveway from the road were massed lilac bushes that promised a glory in the spring.

Here, in this beautiful place, we settled to a lotus-land existence, the central purpose of which was to restore Denby to perfect health.

I was as happy as it was possible for me to be without Robert. He did not write and neither did I, but every six weeks a letter came from his office written in the neat copper-plate of an office clerk, telling me about my mother's health and whereabouts — if she was in London, or touring, and meticulously setting out her financial affairs and the monies paid to her. It was signed with Robert's strong, flourishing signature. I kept these letters, and sometimes looked at that name, Robert Thornton, and secretly laid my lips against it, foolishly, but that was all.

I never wrote to Rollers Croft, but Denby wrote often to his mother, requesting English books, tea, and various small things for our comfort to be sent out. He told her, for he showed me the letters, how much his health had improved and how devotedly I cared for him.

He had many letters from Jonathan about the estate, papers for his signature and requests for permission over various matters. To sell the lease of the house in Farm Street, as the family was never in London now, to buy more land, to increase the mineral interests as the mining industry grew in Derbyshire.

I heard from Felicia occasionally. Brief letters, tinged with sadness. 'Jonathan works as though some awful fate would overtake him if he stopped,' she wrote. 'I think that night when Denby was shot is a nightmare that comes back to him. Sometimes he drinks too much, and rides too hard across the open dales. His mother too is quiet, broods, entertains very little — and I try to serve them both, to love them, but cannot make them happy.'

'Jonathan is a great man of business now,' Denby said after one of these letters. 'It must be bitter for him, and I am sorry for him. We were close in spite of the rivalry between us. He should have been the heir — but I cannot regret anything, for what happened brought you to me. I have you, whom we both wanted so much — but at times I feel an idle creature, living here with my beautiful wife in this quiet paradise.'

We were sitting on the terrace in the evening. Shortly some neighbours of ours would come and we would have the light sparkling wine from Asti served with sweetmeats and little ratafia biscuits, and for our English friends and ourselves tea which we had especially sent out from London. Perhaps Denby would play on the fine harpsichord in the salon and I would sing, or if there were English people there, recite some of the speeches from Shakespeare that I knew. Denby made no attempt to hide the fact that I had been an actress, and loved to display my talent.

Sometimes we went into Genoa, to the opera or to *conversaziones* held in one of the black and white marble *palazzos*. We had many letters of introduction to Genoese society which seemed to me either poor and very noble, or rich and mercantile. I was amused by the ladies, so shy and demure as young girls, so vivacious and flirtatious when married, with their *cavaliera serventi* dancing attendance almost as a matter of convention.

True to his word Denby had bought me very many beautiful things, velvets, laces, silks, and gauzes which I had made up by the cheap and clever Genoese dressmakers, and in the jewellers' shops he bought corals, cameos, gold and pearls. This evening I was wearing a gown of lavender gauze with a full and flowing line which had recently become fashionable, and cameos of pale pink coral. Every gold-framed oval contained a miniature sculpture of god or goddess, cupid and satyr. We had examined them through a magnifying glass in the shop, and had marvelled at their beauty and accuracy. They had been the first present Denby had bought me.

'What more can anyone want but this?' he said happily.

I looked round at all the beauty, but restlessness stirred in me. All my adult life I had worked, the hard work and strict discipline, the constant learning of the stage. I said, unthinkingly, 'I would like something to do — some kind of work, Denby. I am used to being occupied.'

A shadow crossed his face. 'You are not happy?'

I said quickly, 'I am not unhappy, but I am idle ...'

He said teasingly, 'You must be the only lady in Genoa without a *cavaliere*, Sarah. Shall we find you a handsome young man to dance and promenade with like the other ladies?'

'No,' I said angrily, 'I do not want admirers ... I want no one else but you.'

A shadow crossed his face, and he said, 'No one? No one else at all. Are you sure, Sarah?'

Something in his voice made me look up, and I said perhaps too quickly, 'Of course I'm sure.'

I do not know exactly when it was I began to notice that he was not quite so well. At first it was so gradual, like the warmth of the summer slipping away. One did not really notice it as one did not notice the chill dawn wind or the sudden spatter of rain. It was so little — nothing really. An increasing desire to stay within doors, but then we had the mistral for some days, and on another, the *tramontana* — the bleak wind that blows down from the Alpine snows. A yellowness about his skin as the suntan of summer faded, the deepening shadows about his eyes. One day, going into the garden to call him into dinner I saw him coming slowly up the marble steps to the terrace, pausing on each step as though the effort was immense. He looked up and saw me, and when I ran down to him, put his arm across my shoulders, and said, 'I'm not so well, Sarah — perhaps we should move farther south now that the summer has gone. Perhaps to Naples?'

'Perhaps you should see a doctor,' I said firmly. 'Why did you not tell me you felt so tired?'

I was standing on the step above him and suddenly he put his fair head down on my shoulder like a weary child. 'I am a poor husband for such a lovely wife,' he said. 'I did so want to be strong again. For a while I felt my beastly health had mended . . . now, I am not sure.'

All the compassion I had always felt for him rose in my heart. I lifted his face and kissed his lips, and said, 'It will — I know it will. We will find the best doctor in the city, and get him to prescribe.'

The best doctor in the city, recommended by a contessa, arrived — a yellow-faced little man with sharp black eyes and rather confused English. He examined Denby carefully, and then said, 'Nothing to worry, nothing to worry.' The bedroom had a fragrant wood fire stacked with pine cones but outside the trees were creaking in the cold wind. *Molto fredo, molto fredo*,' he said, and then banging his hollow chest, '*Molto tossa?* Much cough?'

'No, my husband does not cough much,' I said.

'No? Ah, well, I make the prescription.'

I followed him downstairs, and his affable and charming manner changed as soon as we were out of Denby's hearing. 'I do not like,' he said, 'I do not like at all. I would know more of your husband's history. He has been so ill before?'

'He has always been delicate — and as you could see, he was seriously wounded in an accident . . .'

'It is not the wound,' he said. 'That is nothing. It is quite healed. Have you no one you could write to in England?'

I remembered the doctor in Sheffield, Dr. Granger.

'Yes. But it will take some time — some weeks before I can get a reply.'

'Please do this. *Informazione* we must have. *Va bene!* I will wait to hear with interest. *Arriverderci*, Baronessa.'

I went back to Denby who was sitting at his desk — I went in quietly, and was disturbed by his despondent attitude, head upon his hands. He looked up as I approached, and raised his head.

'What did he say?'

'He said you would soon be well,' I told him, but for the first time since we married, I was afraid for him.

I wrote to Dr. Granger, telling him what had happened, and asking him to write to me as soon as possible. A month or six weeks passed, the winter rains set in, and then cleared to a high bright sunshine, warm at midday, but cold at nights. We bought warm clothes in the city, and in the evenings sat in my small parlour before a big fire. Our relationship had passed into that of a sister and brother, it was weeks since Denby had made love to me. He did not seem any worse, though not particularly better — just lassitude and lack of energy, and he complained sometimes of aches in his joints, and bruised easily, although he could not remember knocking himself.

It was well over a month before I received Dr. Granger's reply. I was horrified. He said he had suspected that Denby suffered from a dangerous type of pernicious anaemia, and that he had warned Lady Charlotte about it and had also told her to inform me if Denby and I were going to marry and he was distressed that I had not been warned. He said that he had never known a case recover, although sometimes they lived for some long time, sometimes appeared to have partial recovery. From what I had told him it seemed to him that Denby had entered a period of decline.

I was terribly distressed. It did not matter that Lady Charlotte had not told me; in the mood I had been in after the shooting I would have married him in any case. But I was glad that Denby did not know and knew I must make him as well and happy as was in my power.

The doctor was with him that morning, and I waited for him to come down into the hall. He called regularly, saw Denby in his room and I usually offered him a glass of wine in the salon while he talked to me before going away.

When he came I showed him Dr. Granger's letter — he

picked the meaning out slowly, nodding in agreement, shaking his head, and then looked up at me, his sharp black eyes full of compassion.

'Baronessa, life is difficult and we must do the best. It is a tragedy that this should happen to so young a man, so rich, so happy...'

'But — is it true? Is his *life* in danger?' I was aghast. 'For God's sake, Doctor Lipati?'

'I think — I think he will see the bambino, Baronessa ... I would tell him now — it would be wise. All men are happy to know there is a child coming. Perhaps it will make him get better? There are always miracles, Baronessa, if we have the faith.'

He looked into my astounded eyes and said gently, 'Did you not know? Had you not guessed? On my first visit I saw your face, the look of youth that goes for a small while. The baby he steals it for a time — he makes the little *piazzas* here ...' He spread his thin brown fingers across his cheek bones, and I knew at once what he meant. I had noticed the flat patches of faded colour on my usually glowing cheeks. I had noticed but barely thought about the change in body and face, and perhaps because I had experienced no depth of delight in Denby's lovemaking I had not thought it would result in this. 'You mean — I am going to have a child?'

'But, yes, *bella signora*. In the spring. He will see his child, and as I said, who knows, miracles happen, perhaps it will make him want more to live. More strong to live.'

I locked the letter from Dr. Granger away in my writing-desk and went in to see Denby, who rose, his face full of anxious query, a little startled by my radiant face.

'What is it?' Hope sprang into his eyes. 'Did he say I was better?'

'Yes,' I lied. 'He is very pleased with you,' and then I told him my news, hoping it would make him happy. 'And he told me we are to have a child.'

A strange expression crossed his face as he put his arms about me, of joy and triumph, but sorrow too.

'What is it, Denby? Are you not happy?'

'Happy — I am so happy, Sarah. It was something I had not dreamed of. But Jonathan? If we have a boy, Sarah, he will come before Jonathan, whatever happens to me.'

I put my arms round him. I said determinedly, 'Nothing is going to happen to you.'

But from that moment I prayed with all my heart that my baby would be a girl.

All through that winter and the following spring we lived quietly and were extraordinarily happy together. I think we both knew, although we never mentioned it, that Denby would not recover, and because of this there was a kind of passionate devotion to each other, to make these days happy and worthwhile.

The Italian doctor proved correct — the beautiful Italian spring had come, and the lilacs, white, mauve and dark purple tossed along the driveway filling the air with their perfume, the roses and bougainvilia dripped over the terraces — and my baby daughter was born, early one perfect morning, with little yellow Dr. Lipati and my dear Ridstone in attendance.

'*Una picolina ragazza dell'argenta*. A little silver girl,' he said when he gave her to Mrs. Ridstone to wash. He looked at me doubtfully. 'She is welcome, Baronessa? I so hope. For I think there will be no more bambini . . . no boy . . .'

'My husband is worse?' I asked anxiously, for I had begun to hope that with the warm and lovely weather Denby would mend again.

He shook his head, and shrugged, and said, 'No — no worse. But no better, Baronessa. You must be prepared.'

We called her Stella, for she was our star of hope, and she *was* a little silver baby, so fair that the down on her head was invisible, only glinting when the sun caught it. She was strong and well, and I was so happy. I had a girl, with no claim to property, title or estate. My girl whom I would love and rear to be without envious ambition.

Denby when he came looked at us with eyes full of love, and knelt beside me, and put his head against my breast, and I felt at peace for that moment, knowing that I had done what I had longed to do — repaired some of the harm I had caused with joy.

One day, about two weeks later, when I was up and about again, after Dr. Lipati had made his weekly call, Denby went for a walk along the mountain lanes behind the house. It was a way we often went, not too steep, winding along through an old walled village, and on beside a torrent, dried in the summer, but in the winter, cutting steeply through the olive orchards and round the vine terraces. The mountains were beautiful, with broom like huge yellow butterflies and small purple mountain flowers everywhere.

I did not go — how often afterwards did I blame myself that I did not go, but it was a short while since Stella's birth, and I still tired easily. I knew he would not go far as within a mile the way grew too steep and exhausting for him. He came in, carrying his big sunhat of fine straw, and kissed us both before he went. It was the last time he kissed me.

When two hours passed I began to get nervous, and after another hour, I sent two men from the estate to search for him. They carried him home on a hurdle. They had found him far up the mountain, along a rough steep path, where only the sturdy goatherds went. He had fallen, but not a high or serious fall. He had just gone on, pushing his fading strength to collapse. He was dead from heart failure.

When Dr. Lipati came his face was serious and sad. He told me that when he had called earlier, Denby had Dr. Granger's letter. Apparently he had bought me a pendant, a beautiful carved angel's skin coral to celebrate Stella's birth, set in diamonds, and had thought to put it into my jewellery case as a surprise. He had opened it and found the letter. He had wondered all through the year why he did not recover, and this was the answer. When the doctor came he had confronted him with the letter and demanded the truth.

'He said to me, Baronessa, he said, "She has the baby, and we are now so happy ... why should she be burdened with sorrow, sickness and death?" He asked how it would be with him. when the end came, and I said it would be a very slow decline, not to make worries, sometimes he would feel most well ... but he shook his head, and smiled.'

Dr. Lipati took my hand, for I could not speak, and said,

'*Bella signora*, all the time the Baron speak to me, he seem most happy...'

I found the jewel in my case, and Dr. Granger's letter and written across the bottom of it the words in Denby's fine, sloping script, 'Thank you, my darling, for this most wonderful year.'

CHAPTER EIGHT

Denby was buried in the little English cemetery in the city. I and Dr. Lipati, my dear Mrs. Ridstone, and one or two friends and neighbours whom we had come to know during the past year followed him to his resting-place. I felt queer and calm, not yet wakened from the dream that this strange, unreal year had been for me. But there was baby Stella, my treasure, my comforting little reality.

I wrote letters and sent them by express mail to Lady Charlotte and Jonathan — Sir Jonathan now — and also to Robert and my mother, telling them of Denby's death and that I was travelling back to England immediately.

Dr. Lipati was a good friend to me, and found a fast schooner bound for the port of London which was to leave Genoa at once. I did not want to travel the long journey overland with a young baby, for although the French wars had been over some time, the roads were not safe. Bands of freebooters, demobilised soldiers, roamed France still, and there were many bandits in the Italian mountains. But by sea with good weather I would be back home within a matter of weeks.

Home. England. I had not realised how much I had missed it during my dreamlike stay in our Italian lotus land, and I was beset with impatience to get away, to see England again, my dear mother, and Robert, although I did not let myself think of him.

Many things might have happened. He might have forgotten me although I would never forget him. I was no longer the impetuous girl who had once so helplessly acknowledged her love for him. The past year had taught me a great deal in tolerance, patience and discretion.

Mrs. Ridstone and I packed and I closed the villa, and on a stifling July day we sailed out of the port of Genoa on our way back to England.

When I looked back at the receding land I could make out the high coastal road with its villas like white dots against the mountains, but it was too far to pick out the Casa di Lillas where my brief, strange marriage had blossomed into a quiet happiness and so quickly ended. It was not yet a year since I had married Denby. Whatever happened in the years to come I was leaving a little bit of my life up there in the white house above the sea.

It was a cool, blowy day, with scudding grey clouds when we took the river pilot aboard and came slowly up the river to the London docks.

I stood by Mrs. Ridstone on the deck and we looked at each other and smiled. The cool summer day, the muted cloud shadows racing across the Essex flats, the farmhouses and fat cattle, the windmills, and later the crowded wharfs of Rotherhithe — all spoke of home. I put my arms round her, and said, 'Ridstone, my dear, don't leave me yet ... stay with me if you can. We have been through so much together, and the future is so uncertain. I shall need a good friend.'

We both cried a little, and she blew her nose, and dabbed at her rosy cheeks and dried her eyes, and set her new Italian straw bonnet to rights, and said I was not to talk a lot of nonsense; that although she wanted to see her folk around the Hall, she had no intention of leaving me.

We anchored in midstream below the Tower, and all the panorama of the London river was silhouetted against the sunset. Boats were setting out from the shore, bringing people to meet passengers, and merchants to claim and inspect cargo. I looked across the water to the wharf, while Mrs. Ridstone carried Stella, walking her up and down the busy deck. And then I saw Robert sitting in a wherry, being rowed rapidly out to us. I raised my hand and waved, and he saw me, and stood, baring his head until presently the boat came alongside and we looked at each other intently, searching each other's faces, and my heart chilled, for in that handsome clear-cut face, which I had last seen alight with passionate love for me, was no real welcome or no real warmth.

He came aboard and walked across the deck to me, raising his hat. 'Lady Sarah Sefton,' he said formally, 'I hope you have had a good voyage home.'

I do not know what I had expected — certainly not that we should resume on that wild recognition of love with which we had parted. A year had passed and much had happened; for me marriage, motherhood and with Denby a kind of tender loving. I did not know what that year had held for Robert, but I had not expected this distant formality.

He told me that he had hired the wherry to take us to the Tower steps where a carriage waited for us to drive me to my mother's rooms in Grays Inn Road.

'Robert,' I protested, 'you are very formal. Are you not glad to see me again? And do you expect me to call you Mr. Thornton?'

He shook his head, and his face relaxed a little. 'I expect nothing from you, Sarah, other than to be yourself.'

'Come, that is better. This is my daughter, Stella.'

He looked at the baby in the way men of affairs who have never had anything to do with them always look — at least English men do. Dr. Lipati could handle a baby like a woman. Somewhere I felt a touch of laughter, and said, 'Sure, and she won't eat you, Robert.'

'You sound like your mother,' he said, and put out one of his long fingers which Stella immediately grasped and favoured him with a toothless, windy smile, which seemed to surprise him as much as though she had spoken. He retrieved his finger.

'How is my mother?' I asked.

'She is well and greatly looking forward to seeing you.' He touched my arm, the merest touch, and turned me away from Mrs. Ridstone. 'Shall we walk while the trunks are unloaded?'

142

We walked along the deck leaving Mrs. Ridstone holding Stella, but keeping watch over our luggage as it was lowered by pulley into the wherry below.

'Sarah, I must tell you that some time ago before the baby was born I had a letter from Denby asking me to act for you and the baby should anything happen to him. He also sent me his will, duly witnessed by a Dr. Lipati and an English friend in Florence. He has made me the child's guardian with yourself. He left you all his private money, which is not a great deal, and asked me to act jointly with you as the child's guardian. The body of the estate as you and your mother have reason to know is entailed, so that now Sir Jonathan is in possession of the estate, lands and fortune.'

'But I am glad about this,' I said quickly. 'I have no intention of going to Rollers Croft. My mother has her income from my father, Gerard Danjou, and there is also the small capital I left from my earnings on the stage, which you have looked after so well. I am grateful to you for that.'

'It is little enough, Sarah.'

'It is enough if we live modestly. We can move in with my mother in Grays Inn Road, or perhaps later find a small house just outside London. I had thought to work again — my mother has said that Mr. MacFarren and Mr. Hodgson of the Royalty would welcome me back. I cannot tell you, Robert, how grateful I am that my baby is a girl. She is mine, and I can bring her up with love, and there will be no involvement with the Seftons.'

'I must tell you, Sarah, that I have had a letter from Lady Charlotte saying that Sir Jonathan would be glad if you will proceed to Rollers Croft as soon as is convenient to you after your journey. And that, as your lawyer, they would be obliged if you would permit me to accompany you.'

I went white.

'Robert — they have no claim on my baby? They could not take her away from me? Why should they want to see her now?'

'I imagine,' he said quietly, 'Lady Charlotte wishes to see her only grandchild. I cannot speak for Sir Jonathan.'

'He has the baronetcy now. The house, the lands, the mines

and the money. It is what he always wanted. Why should he want to see my baby? I won't go.'

'Sarah, you have no need to be afraid. The Seftons have no possible legal right to Stella. But I am her joint guardian, and I am also her lawyer. That she will be happy with you and your mother, I do not doubt. But there are material things too . . . Sir Jonathan is very wealthy — if he wishes to make any kind of settlement on the child, or on yourself, this would only be his duty. And it would be my duty to request it.'

'I would rather you did not.'

'You can instruct me to that effect if you wish.'

'I do.'

'But not so far as the child is concerned. You are young and a woman of great beauty and fascination, Sarah. You do not know what life holds for you. You had the experience of being deprived and rejected as a child . . .'

'But it was not my heritage. Gerard Danjou was my father, not Sir Gore, you told me yourself.'

'But you did not know that then, and neither did Lady Charlotte. She does not know now. Your little Stella's case is quite different. She is Denby's legal daughter . . . it is my duty to see her interests are protected.'

'Is this why my friend has vanished?' I asked, the turbulent tears springing to my eyes. 'And you have become this cold man of law? Are you no longer interested in how I *feel* . . . only in what is right and just and legal?'

'At the moment, I have no choice.'

'But all this could be settled through your office. There is no need for me to take Stella to Rollers Croft.'

'It might be kind of you to do so. Lady Charlotte has aged greatly, and kindness has never been evident between you. Sir Denby was her son, and I believe she feels remorse because she preferred the other boy . . . so her letter suggests. Your husband was only a boy, Sarah, very young to die. I think you should control your pride and your fear and make this one concession. You need not stay many days.'

'You will come with me?'

'Yes.'

'And you swear they have no claim to her?'

'Yes.'

'Very well. In a few days. We will go to my mother's apartment as we had planned, and when we are a little settled, I will visit Rollers Croft again.'

But I did not want to go. It hung over me like some oppressive cloud. I did not want to see Lady Charlotte and I dreaded meeting Jonathan. I remembered his pursuit of me that year in London, when I could not turn without seeing those narrow blue eyes burning at me wherever I went and the tall, good-looking, broad-shouldered figure, moving near me along the streets or in the green room; the bouquets, the returned gifts, the attempted seductions.

My mother created a great and joyful fuss at our arrival and to my astonishment she had been most efficient in her arrangements — she had engaged another room for Mrs. Ridstone and Stella, there was even a baby's cot ready. Everything was newly decorated and fresh and pretty. But when I congratulated her, she said in her old way, 'Well, to tell you the truth, Alannah, as soon as Mr. Thornton knew you were coming back with that blessed baby, he had Mrs. Billings re-doing and redecorating as though the queen herself was coming, and very nice it is too.'

She sat cuddling and crooning to Stella as though she had never had a baby out of her arms for the twenty-one years since I was born. She glanced across at me in the old anxious way, and went on, 'There's no shadow of doubt, Sally, that Mr. Thornton thinks the very world of you, and now you are a widow so to speak...'

'Mother!' I spoke in my old reprimanding way which had been a habit of mine when I was the bread earner, and kept her firmly in order. 'That's quite sufficient. Mr. Thornton has other things to see to — at the moment I have no more intention of marrying than — than you have yourself.'

'Well, now you mention it, my darlin', I have been going to write to you, but you know that writing comes very badly to me, and I felt it must come directly from myself, you see...'

'Mama, what *are* you trying to tell me?' I demanded. 'That you are married again?'

'Well, no, not exactly, Sally. But I have been offered for.' She drew herself up and her plump, pretty face bridled a little at my astonishment. 'And why not? Sure, I'm still on the right side of fifty, and I'll have you know that he's not the only one who has cast an eye in my direction this past year.'

I literally gaped at her, my mouth open with astonishment. It was the last thing I had expected. But I could well see that with the security, the money Gerard Danjou had left her, the awful anxiety of poverty, and the gnawing worrying of having to face up to life had gone. She had changed. Well-dressed, smooth, sleek and charming in her plump, pretty, blarneying way she was a very attractive middle-aged woman.

'And who, may I ask, is this impassioned suitor?'

'Ah, get away with you, you and your sarcastic tongue. Sure you had your own prettiness from me, for Gerard was a brown creature, and you've nothing from him but your temper and your green eyes. Don't be pretending I'm past all loving.'

I melted, because I was near to laughter. She was irrepressible.

'Mama, darling, please.'

'Well, who should it be but Mr. MacFarren? Well, why not? He's Dublin born, like myself, and been a player for as long as he can remember, like myself. I have some nice parts with him — just enough, not too much work. And it's the life I know, touring and playing. I understand it well. If I'd had any sense in my head at all, I should have married a player when I was a girl, not gone off with aristocrats. Gerard and Sir Gore .... what good did either of them do me? A bit of spoiling, as though I was a plaything, and a lot of rage and fuss and tragedy. Better if I'd never met the two of them, then none of our troubles would have happened.'

'But, Mama darling, neither would I have happened — nor Stella.'

'Well, in Mary's blessed name,' she said in astonishment, 'I never thought of that . . .' and I was across the room, my arms round her, and we were laughing together as we often had in the old days, in the dressing-room, when something droll had set us off.

Robert did not call to see me during the next few days, and my mother was absorbed with Stella, carrying her round for all the neighbours to admire, and even taking her in a hackney to the theatre so that Mr. MacFarren and his Shakespearean company could be amazed at her beauty and cleverness which Herself assured everyone was quite unique in a baby of this age, although my daughter's accomplishments consisted only of waving her pink fists and making rather rude noises. But my mother returned bearing her granddaughter in triumph.

'And didn't MacFarren himself say she was as beautiful as her mama and her grandma, and that we'd all live to see her play Juliet, and him toasting her in champagne and her laughing and smiling at them all. Sure it was like a first night for my little lady, and . . .'

'Yes, Mama,' I interrupted, rescuing my now hiccuping child, 'I'm sure she is the most beautiful child in the world but I hope you didn't give her any champagne . . .' I gave Baby to Mrs. Ridstone to change and feed, and my mother looked round and asked if Robert had been there.

'No,' I answered her shortly.

'I cannot understand it — I ask because I saw him in Holborn and stopped the carriage to show him the baby.'

'He has seen the baby, Mother.'

'Until you came home he called here always once a week, to see if I needed anything at all, and sat talking for half an hour.'

'What about?'

'What about? About you, for sure. Nothing else. He would read your letters to me, for as you know, with my eyes, I'm a poor hand at reading . . .' she never would admit she could not read. 'All your letters he read to me every week . . .'

The colour flooded up my cheeks, for although I knew someone would have to read her my letters I had not thought it would be Robert. I had told her a great deal of my life with Denby, of his gentle consideration, and my growing anxieties for him, and my distress when I had found how grave his illness really was. Somehow I felt that I had exposed my heart too much in this record of my progress from a guilty sense of duty towards Denby to a sincere and anxious affection. In Italy I had determinedly put Robert out of my heart and mind or I might have been unable to do what I set out to do. To make Denby happy.

'You must have done something to offend him,' she said decidedly, 'for him to change so much.'

I was beginning to understand what had happened between us. It is difficult for a man to say he no longer loves a woman, particularly a man like Robert. He would have to be blunt and honest and kind. He was not a ruthless man like Jonathan Sefton, pursuing and discarding as his fancy took him. Nor would he pretend to a love he no longer felt for me.

'A year is a year,' I said, 'I am not the only woman Robert Thornton knows. Perhaps he has found someone else.'

But that very day a letter came from him from his office, businesslike and formal. He had been in communication with Lady Charlotte, and I could manage it he would like to make the journey to Rollers Croft Hall the following day. If I wished to stay on, I could do so, but he would return to London at the weekend. I sent Mrs. Ridstone round to his office with an equally formal note saying I would be ready at the time arranged.

If I had thought that the long journey to Derby with Robert would be an embarrassment to me, I was quite wrong. Whatever Robert felt, or whatever emotions he was concealing, he was too urbane and too much a man of the world to allow it to intrude upon our relationship. We travelled in Sefton splendour — Sir Jonathan had sent his carriage down for us and it was arranged for me to spend the night at the Talbot Inn at Stamford where rooms had been reserved. If this evening brought any memories back to Robert of our first meeting in the stage-coach to London, when he had so charmingly entertained my mother and myself, he made no reference to it.

He was, as always, highly efficient in making arrangements for my comfort. Mrs. Ridstone and I were given good rooms with a sitting-room, to which our dinner was brought. Robert courteously excused himself — he had, he said, an engagement to dine with a client in the district.

After we had put Stella to bed and dined, I told Mrs. Ridstone that I would go out for a little while to see the town, for there were some interesting old buildings there, and I needed some air. It was a warm, light summer evening. I felt restless and very apprehensive about this return to Rollers Croft Hall.

I put on my bonnet — I was still in mourning, but my black dress was of fine Italian mousseline, and I had a large triangle of black silk lace which I wore mantilla-like over my bonnet and shoulders.

It was a long time since I had walked abroad in a town alone: in Italy it was not permissible, but I had not considered that, in this provincial town, I would appear outstandingly elegant and rich. I had become so accustomed to dressing very well, and wearing jewellery. My theatrical training too had given me assurance — I walked, as Jonathan Sefton had once told me, like a young queen. These things were natural to me, and it had not entered my head that I would be a very conspicuous figure walking through the dusk, with the rural folk and the riff-raff of the day's market, gypsies, touts and hucksters still about the streets. I had gone some way before I realised that I was being followed by three young men, the rough, burly, idle sort, and the sort that hang about fairgrounds and street corners. They followed, guffawing among themselves, a few yards behind, so I had to turn and face them or hurry onwards, finding my way back to the inn by another way.

I had been in worse situations, but then I had been a poorly dressed young actress, with no valuables — now I was uncomfortably conscious of my rings, my long gold chain with the pendant which had been Denby's last present. I hurried on uneasily ... It was then I passed a small tavern. The doors stood wide on this warm summer night, and I instantly recognised the figure sitting at the rough deal table, alone, hatless, head on hands — I should have known that thick dark hair with the startling white wing anywhere.

I called unhesitatingly, 'Robert!'

In an instant he looked up, saw my plight and was by my side. At his tall, imposing presence my followers vanished.

I said, apologetically, 'Robert, I always seem to turn to you when I am in a scrape.'

'It might be better if you did not wear expensive gold chains when walking abroad in the dusk.'

'I did not think. It is so long since I went out alone. In England I thought it would be safe enough.'

'Except that it is late, and has been market day, when many rough travelling folk get into the town.' He replaced his hat and offered me his arm. 'I will walk you back to the Talbot.'

I accepted, and we walked in silence for a while, then I could not resist saying, 'Did you dine with your important client in that tavern?'

'No,' he said stiffly, 'the — er the meeting was cancelled. I dined alone. I did not want a meal — I had some bread and cheese and a pint of ale.'

I was sure there had been no client in Stamford.

'You mean you wanted an excuse not to dine with me?'

He looked down on my hand where it lay on the broad-cloth of his sleeve, and for a moment I thought he would put his other hand over it, as he had sometimes done when we walked together in the past, but he did not.

'You are a young widow,' he said, 'a very beautiful young widow ... indeed in black, Sarah, your fairness shines like a pearl ...' I waited, and my heart began to race, but he went on firmly, 'Sir Jonathan asked me to accompany you to Rollers Croft, but I did not think this included dining with you. He might object to that.'

My mother's Irish temper flared. 'I have not made this journey to please Sir Jonathan. I have only come because you pressed me to let Lady Charlotte see her grandchild. What I choose to do or not to do is no business of Sir Jonathan's.'

'You had better wait until you have seen him before you decide on that.'

'I hope I do not see him. But I am tired of this absurd formality, Robert. If you do not wish to remember — or do not wish *me* to remember any —' I hesitated — 'any feeling that was between us in the past, I understand. But you did say once you were my lawyer and my friend. I am seeing too much of the lawyer and too little of the friend.'

We had reached the entrance porch of The Talbot, and I

went up the steps thinking he would follow me. But he stood on the pavement, making no attempt to do so. He stood, with his hat in his hand, his handsome head bent, not meeting my eyes. He said, expressionlessly, 'I think it is scarcely possible for us to be friends at this moment, Sarah.'

'But why?' I said aghast. I felt he was deserting me.

'Because the girl who sailed to Genoa a year ago is quite different from the magnificent young woman who has returned.' He put on his hat, and added quickly, 'If you will excuse me I will leave now. I am not staying here — I am staying at the small tavern where you saw me in the bar. I will be ready early in the morning to continue our journey. I wish you good night, Sarah.'

I went slowly upstairs to my room. Mrs. Ridstone was sitting in the window bay knitting. She was looking forward to seeing her folks in Derbyshire again, for she had been bred and born on the estate at Rollers Croft. I bade her good night and went into my own room, where Stella lay asleep in a cot. He would not even stay under the same roof as myself on this journey. I looked at the sleeping baby, so silkily fair and pink, like a small round apple-blossom bud. Perhaps she was all I had now.

We arrived at Rollers Croft Hall early the following evening. I saw it from the top of the slope as the carriage went along the drive, but now it brought me no feelings of longing or pride. A big country house that had nothing to do with me. I noticed how well everything was tended, hedges, grass and sleek cattle, and remarked upon it.

'Sir Jonathan is an excellent estate manager,' said Robert, 'and an acute man of business. His wildness was I think merely the frustration of being the second son — he certainly looked after things well here. And invested wisely. You must remember that baby in your arms *might* have been a son, and in that case he would have received a splendid heritage.'

I shrugged. 'Well, thank the Lord then that she is just my Stella,' I replied.

The carriage drew up to the portico and a butler came out, and running behind him, as though she had been watching for us, Felicia. She had changed. The plump pretty girl had become a tall, slender young woman. The eyes were just as blue, and the curly brown hair as luxuriant. But there was a new quality about her, a wistful resignation, which I could not quite understand.

She came towards me as soon as I descended from the carriage. She was wearing a dress of black gauze over a dark grey undergown, and I realised that she too was in mourning for Denby.

'Cia,' I said, 'how pretty you look. Are you well?'

'Oh, yes, well enough. I've grown thin, haven't I?' Without waiting for any comment she turned to the baby who was in Mrs. Ridstone's arms. 'Oh, here she is. Oh, Sarah, how sweet! How lovely! Ridstone, it is good to see you again. Your daughter Gilly has been waiting in the kitchen for you for the past hour ... She has the children with her. Ridstone may go and see her, mayn't she, Sarah?'

'Of course,' I said, and Mrs. Ridstone went off through the baize-lined service door. 'Cia, this is my lawyer, Mr. Robert Thornton.'

'Oh, yes.' Felicia made a small, indifferent curtsy and Robert bowed. She had taken Stella from Mrs. Ridstone and was now looking down at her eagerly. 'Aunt Charlotte and I have been longing to see her. It will be wonderful to have a baby here at Rollers Croft. We have been very dull since ... Well, since your marriage ... neither my aunt nor Jonathan care for company now. Come, I will take you to Lady Charlotte ...'

Still carrying my daughter she set off quickly across the black and white marble floor along the corridor towards Lady Charlotte's little parlour, leaving us in the Hall. I glanced at Robert in terror as she disappeared round a corner, and he shook his head and smiled, and for the first time I felt a warm human reassurance in his manner.

The butler took charge of us.

'If you will come this way, m'Lady — and Mr. Thornton, Lady Charlotte is expecting you.'

He led the way — it was the same man who had so superciliously shown me the door all those years ago, when I was sixteen and had come here with such foolish and desperate hopes. Quite obviously he did not recognise me.

We followed him and were presently shown into the room which I remembered so well. The room which had been my mother's pretty, rosy haven, and which Lady Charlotte had altered. It was exactly the same as when I had last seen it. Dark and rather gloomy with red brocade, dominated by the portrait of the two small boys, one fair, fine-drawn and delicate, the other sturdy and strong, brown-haired, sternly admonishing a fawning hound. Denby and Jonathan.

There was a small fire in the grate in spite of the warm day, and Lady Charlotte sat in a high-back chair. I was shocked by the change in her. Her black hair was now quite white and she seemed to have aged in this single year. She too was in black — I found it unbearably oppressive — we three black-garbed women in this over-heated red and gold room.

Felicia went swiftly across and placed my baby on her grandmother's knee.

'Here she is, Aunt Charlotte. Den's little girl. Is she not very sweet?'

Lady Charlotte touched the baby's cheek.

'She is so fair. Like Denby.'

'A little silver girl, the Italian doctor called her,' I said, and heard a stir behind me. Jonathan was standing there. He had been standing in the shadow behind the door as we came in so I had not seen him.

He looked older, much older than his twenty-four years. He seemed thin, though still very handsome in the cold fierce way that had been so repellent to me. His unsmiling face and narrow blue eyes seemed drawn by an inner suffering. As though he had been haunted by the memory of that night when he had tried to kill me and would have done if Denby had not stood in his way.

I made a small obeisance, and said, 'Sir Jonathan.'

I saw the colour flush up in his face and, with a sense of shock, knew I had hurt him. I had never thought it possible to do such a thing. I realised that the title which he had so longed to possess was a burden and a reproach to him now.

'Sit down, sit down, Sarah,' said Lady Charlotte, 'and you must excuse my not rising. I have not been well this winter.'

Before I did so I took my baby from her knee, and unloosed her shawl, for her little face was becoming quite red in the hot room. I undid my bonnet strings and put back my lace mantilla, and sat there, facing them, with my baby resting against my breast.

'Why have you sent for me?' I said.

She looked at me with terrible humility.

'We are asking your forgiveness now, Sarah,' she said. 'I did not tell you that Denby had not long to live when I implored you to marry him. I was full of guilt, and so were you for what had happened. But you made his life so happy and I am deeply grateful. Every letter I had from him from Italy confirmed this. Jonathan and I know that although he made provision for you it is very little . . .'

'Lady Charlotte,' I interrupted, 'you owe me nothing. Just after I married Denby I learned the truth about my parenthood. Gerard Danjou was my father, not Sir Gore as I had always been led to believe. I have never had any claim on you at all. I do not wish you to help me in any way. I am quite capable of providing for myself.'

Jonathan moved round the back of her chair, leaned on it, and they both looked at me.

'Stubborn,' said Lady Charlotte, 'stubborn. You were when you came pleading for help, and you are now refusing it. Do you propose to go back to the stage to provide for my granddaughter?'

'I may well do that,' I said gravely, 'and with my care and love she will be better off as a play-actress's child than I was — filled with ambition and false pride by the man whom I believed to be my father. At least she will grow up knowing exactly who she is, and upon whom she can rely.'

'Very well,' she said, and I saw her lips tremble, 'but you cannot prevent us from settling money on the child.'

'No. But that you must decide for yourselves. Mr. Thornton here acts for me. I will not pretend that for a young fatherless girl, some fortune is a protection. I cannot always guarantee she will have me. Accidents happen in life. But I ask you not to offer more than a modestly adequate sum. Mr. Thornton and I are her joint guardians — Denby wished it. I shall ask Mr. Thornton to refuse anything extravagant.'

'As you wish,' she said, and turned her head away. I looked up at Robert, and he nodded gravely in agreement.

Jonathan spoke for the first time.

'Sarah, I have been waiting for you to return. All that happened, all the tragedy and the folly, was because you so wanted to rule this house. You have returned to England a very beautiful woman, and whatever your parentage you would grace Rollers Croft. I wanted you to marry me once — will you marry me now? Denby wanted you to be happy. It was my fault that he died. For his sake I would like you to have everything you have ever wanted. I would like you to consider, when a few months have passed, whether you could be my wife after all. My feelings for you are unchanged. I promise neither you nor your little girl would regret it.'

I sat motionless. Here it was. The thing I had fought so hard for and destroyed so much and caused so much unhappiness. I could still have it all if I wished. But now it meant nothing at all. My eyes filled with tears as I held my little girl closely to my breast. I did not care if we always had to live alone or I had to work for the rest of my life on the stage. I wanted none of this.

'Thank you, Jonathan, but no,' I said, and I heard a little sigh behind me, and knew it was Felicia. 'You owe me nothing. Nothing could have helped or cured him. He recovered from the wound, and was well, better than he had ever been. He had a worse enemy than any of us, you or me. No, Jonathan — forget it. Stop reproaching yourself. Pick up your life, and start again . . .' I looked at Robert and to my surprise found his eyes were full of a blazing joy. 'My home and Stella's must be elsewhere.' I put Stella into Felicia's arms while I tied my bonnet strings and the lace over my shoulders.

'Felicia will show you to your room,' said Lady Charlotte.

'No,' I said, 'no, thank you. But I would rather not stay. Stella and I will go back to London now. We will stay the night in Derby, or some nearby town, and travel on in the morning. Mrs. Ridstone will stay, of course, because she has family here whom she has longed to be with. I hope she will return to me, though. She has been a good friend. If you wish Mr. Thornton to stay to attend to whatever you may decide for Stella . . .'

'No,' said Robert authoritatively and he did not take his eyes from me. 'I can return for that or meet Sir Jonathan's representatives in London. I cannot permit you to make the return journey alone.'

'You still hate us so much, Sarah,' said Lady Charlotte unhappily, 'that you will not even spend a night beneath our roof.'

'Ah, no,' I said passionately, 'I have no more hate left for anyone.' I went across to her and knelt by her chair. I took her thin hand in mine. 'No. I will bring Stella here to see you . . . and when she is older, a proper little girl, she can come to stay with you. And then perhaps — ' I smiled up at Jonathan — I was so full of joy I was throwing it round me like a mad sower casting treasured seeds into the wind, 'you will have children of your own. And Stella will have cousins — not like me, imagined cousins. Pretend cousins manufactured out of my own pride and selfishness . . . but real cousins, a real family, and she will stay here and they will play together and get to know and love each other, as families should . . . We will be a real loving family, and forget the past hatred . . .' I rose and held out my arms for my baby, and Felicia gave her back to me. Her pretty face had lost the wistful resignation and sadness and was glowing with a new hope. I kissed her across the baby. I gave my hand to Lady Charlotte, and to my surprise she drew me down and kissed me. I smiled up at Jonathan, surprising for the first time the hint of a smile in those resentful and arrogant eyes. Then I put my hand into Robert's arm and with Stella tucked into my other arm, we went out together.

The carriage was not quite ready. We walked in the gardens until the horses were harnessed. I put Stella down in her shawls in a warm corner on the grass, and Robert and I walked together between the lavender hedges. Across the fields a skylark was circling into the blue singing its triumphant song.

I pulled off my bonnet, and let the wind blow through my hair.

'Well, Robert?' I said.

'I knew he was going to propose marriage,' he said. 'Once it was what you wanted. This young and handsome man, this great title and estate, this fortune. If he had been the eldest you would have married him.'

'Yes,' I said, 'I would have married him — I would have been triumphant.'

'But I had to let you have the chance, Sarah. You are only twenty-one. You have a young child to protect and provide for. Jonathan Sefton is a great prize in the marriage market for any girl be she from the best family in the land. I had to make you come, to listen to him. I know you, Sarah — I know you are impulsive, there is something thoughtlessly generous in you. Once we spoke of love together. If I had spoken of it, you might just from reckless kindness to me not have listened to Jonathan. I am thirty-five, Sarah. I can offer you a good life as my wife. Comfortable, quiet, with modest luxury. But I can offer you nothing compared with this — this house at Rollers Croft — that you once so much desired. In all conscience I could not speak to you first. I had to let you make your own choice.'

I was furiously angry.

'Robert Thornton, how *could* you have done such a thing!' And then, because I was a player and players when their hearts are hurt take refuge in mimickry, I said as Herself might have done in her broad Irish brogue, 'A fig for your conscience. Faith it must have been the divil's got into you, breaking a poor girl's heart for a matter of conscience!' And then, because I could not help it, I burst into tears, and was rewarded by his arms about me, holding me against his shoulder, pressing my face against him so that I could not see that there were tears in his eyes too.

'Dear Robert, marriage between Jonathan and me would have been a disaster. Whether you want it or not, you have to know I love you . . . I want no one else. I never shall.'

'I love you, too. This whole year I have just lived to see you again. And though my heart grieved for that poor boy you married, I could not help hoping and praying that you would one day come back to me.'

We waited for twelve months, and then we were quietly married. Riverbend is now my home. My mother married Mr. MacFarren, and they tour the country, and have been across the ocean to America with their company. We look forward to their visits, and Stella looks forward to their spoiling, but in spite of their blandishments I have no wish or need to go back to the stage again.

Jonathan did marry Felicia — I think in his heart he always wanted to. They have a son now, and occasionally Robert and I travel to Derbyshire to take Stella to see her grandmother. Stella is very lucky in her grandmothers — the darling actress and the great lady. They never meet, of course, but they are both equally good for her.

And now when I sit in the sunshine on the terrace at Riverbend, with my little girl trotting about the garden, and the river shining in the sunshine, waiting for Robert to come from the city, I know there is a new happiness, a new baby within me, Robert's child, and I hope Robert's son — because I would like to be the mother of another such fine, kind and loving man.

I hear the sound of the gig coming into the stable-yard and the white doves flutter in a circle about the lawn and the river. Stella raises one finger and says one of her very first sentences, 'Papa come?'

So I rise and take her hand and we go together to meet him, into his arms which are our home and my kingdom. And I think how fortunate I am that I did not get my coveted dream when I was a reckless, envious, ambitious girl standing, a stranger at the gates of Rollers Croft Hall, all those years ago.

TIME OF DREAMING

JOSEPHINE EDGAR

Encouraged by Dr John Hart, a family friend, Adelina Stirling had decided to train as a nurse. An unconventional heiress, she wanted to escape her wealthy background and her widowed father's protective love. The year was 1899 and already the approaching conflict of the Boer War was casting its shadow over late Victorian England.

But then Addy met the aristocratically handsome Captain Rupert Hop-Dawson and, hoping to see more of him, agreed to do a season with his frivolous sister Anne. Lady Carmina Harborough, a reigning society beauty, successfully engineered Adelina's marriage to the penniless young officer.

All too soon, Rupert was posted to Durban and Addy's time of dreaming was over. She followed him there, hoping to assist at the military hospital established by John Hart to deal with the casualties. And there, amidst the sun-baked hills of South Africa, Addy discovered the true love locked deep in her heart.

CORONET BOOKS

ALSO BY JOSEPHINE EDGAR FROM CORONET BOOKS

☐ 20773 6 THE DANCER'S DAUGHTER   60p

On one dramatic day Bella Bawtry left the fisherman's cottage where she had grown up, to be Miss Isabel Broadbent and live in Sutherdyke Hall. Until her thirteenth year all she knew about herself was that her mother had been a dancer and like everyone else she thought she must be a foundling or a gypsy. But now the truth was out, and she must take up her proper place as a daughter of the Late Sir Lockwood Broadbent and his Spanish wife.

☐ 20775 2 THE DEVIL'S INNOCENTS   60p

Barbara Crossdyke had never overcome her natural shyness, or ventured from the sheltering wing of her father's love. But in the space of one stormy night her tranquil existence was shattered when a handsome young Spaniard, Ramon Ramirez, was carried wounded and unconscious into her home – and into her heart.

All these books are available at your local bookshop or newsagent, or can be ordered direct from the publisher. Just tick the titles you want and fill in the form below.

Prices and availability subject to change without notice.

....

CORONET BOOKS, P.O. Box 11, Falmouth, Cornwall.

Please send cheque or postal order, and allow the following for postage and packing:

U.K. – One book 18p plus 8p per copy for each additional book ordered, up to a maximum of 66p.

B.F.P.O. and EIRE – 18p for the first book plus 8p per copy for the next 6 books, thereafter 3p per book.

OTHER OVERSEAS CUSTOMERS – 20p for the first book and 10p per copy for each additional book.

Name ....

Address ....

....